laptop #3

explosive secrets

Not Everything Lost Is Meant to Be Found

by Christopher P.N. Maselli

Zonderkidz

To Layne Johnson,
my mentor when I was Matt's age.

Zonder**kidz**®

The children's group of Zondervan

www.zonderkidz.com

Explosive Secrets
Copyright © 2003 by Christopher P. N. Maselli

Requests for information should be addressed to:
Grand Rapids, Michigan 49530

ISBN: 0-310-70340-9

Editor: Gwen Ellis
Interior design: Beth Shagene and Todd Sprague
Art direction: Jody Langley

Printed in the United States of America

03 04 05 06 07 08 /❖DC/ 10 9 8 7 6 5 4 3 2 1

Contents

Emergency Break

1

Not long ago, someone made a mistake. And his error, quite divinely, created a breakthrough . . . a breakthrough with too many implications. He should have kept his discovery a secret. Instead, he whispered it into the wrong ear, and it became poison in the hands of a power-hungry deceiver . . . and he became the enemy. This, of course, was never destiny's desire, but sometimes destiny must bend to human demands. For a time.

Ka-thump, ka-thump, ka-thump, ka-thump. Riding in the back of the retired school bus, Matt felt like a can of soda, shaken to the point of explosion. Matt wasn't trying to avoid his dad . . . necessarily . . . he just preferred to sit with his friends. Lamar sat on his right, Gill and Alfonzo on his left. Their fathers all sat at the front of the bus, gabbing about construction and police chases.

"Gimme that!" Gill insisted, pulling the paper out of Matt's hand.

Matt pulled back and ripped the paper down the middle.

"Hey look!" Lamar said with a smile. "Now we have two maps."

Matt shook his head. "This thing's useless anyway. I don't know how we're ever going to find this address."

"I hope we don't," Gill interjected. "Finding that address could be dangerous. And I have to keep myself in perfect condition for my fans."

"Here he goes again." Alfonzo rolled his eyes.

Gill had recently auditioned for a part in a commercial—and two days ago, he had received news that he got the part. Since then, the redhead just knew fame was around the corner. The closer he got to the date of his filming, the more vocal he became.

Gill patted Alfonzo on the head. "When I'm rich and famous, I'll *try* to remember you."

"Oh boy."

Matt held the two pieces of paper together and tried to make sense of the directions. He had printed them from a mapping service on the Internet . . . and found them extremely confusing. "We need a *real* map," Matt muttered. He wasn't sure how they were going to do it, but they just *had* to find that address.

It might even be a matter of life and death.

For his thirteenth birthday, Matt had received a laptop computer because his dad knew how much he liked to write. But this was no ordinary laptop. Whenever he typed a story into it, all he had to do was push a special key with a clock face on it and *bam!* the story became true. Whatever he wrote actually *happened*.

Amazed, Matt and his friends searched the Internet for answers about the laptop's origin, but they only found a few clues. When they ran a search for "Wordtronix," the laptop's brand name, they received two hits: one was a fake company website. The other was a warning. It came up on a white web page with simple black type.

```
If you've come here, then I must be dead
and you must have the Wordtronix. I hope
they don't find you. I've evaded them for
years now, but I know each day their
search intensifies. They want their laptop
back, whatever the cost. Don't be fooled.
Their promises mean nothing. Trust me,
I know. You have power in your hands.

Wield it well ... as long as you can.
```

Just thinking about the cryptic message made Matt shiver. But there was a light at the end of the tunnel: The boys had discovered the message was written by someone named Sam Dunaway, who lived at RR1, Box 87 in Landes, Arizona. And since the address was near their youth group's first annual father/son retreat, Matt was determined to stop by.

"I can't believe you guys really want to find this place," Gill pressed.

"C'mon!" Alfonzo countered. "You need a little adventure in your life!"

Gill's head dropped. "Adventure?! Ever since Matt got the laptop, we've been dodging bullets, fists, and storms. Finding this place could be yet one more life-threatening escapade. This could ruin my career. Don't you remember the warning?!"

"All too well," Matt said, "but that's why we *have* to find this address. I don't want to find out who 'they' are one day by surprise. I want to be ready."

"Ready to get hurt?" Gill asked. "Ready to die?"

Matt scrunched up his face. That was the most ridiculous thing he'd ever heard. "You're not going to die. The worst you'll get is poison ivy."

Gill's jaw popped open and his ears wiggled. *"Poison ivy?!* I could get poison ivy?"

"You're not going to get poison ivy," Lamar calmed Gill, who was already scratching his leg.

Matt looked again at the torn printout in his hand. "Let's see if there's a map up front."

He stood and steadied himself as the bus rolled down the highway. Then he started down the aisle, Lamar on his heels. Eight other boys and their fathers sat scattered throughout the bus. They were headed for the retreat, hoping for "a weekend of fun—camping, playing sports, talking, and seeking the Lord." And Matt couldn't have been less enthusiastic. Sure, a few weeks ago he had begun warming to the idea.

They were headed for the retreat, hoping for "a weekend of fun—camping, playing sports, talking, and seeking the Lord."

He and his dad had been getting along better than ever, and Matt was really enjoying being around him. Then, suddenly, Matt felt like he and his dad were living in different worlds.

Matt noticed it for the first time two weeks prior, when they'd gone to Burger King for a late-night snack. All the way to the fast-food haven, they had chatted about an upcoming Pixar flick. They entered the restaurant and were halfway through placing their order when his dad's phone rang. He "had" to get it—and then proceeded to talk business through almost the entire meal. With every chew, Matt felt more and more upset and disappointed. It wasn't exactly his idea of a rip-roaring good time. Still, it was forgivable; his dad managed several construction sites, and he was very busy. What wasn't as easily forgivable for Matt was when it happened two more times within the same week. Once at the dentist's office and once when they sat down to watch *7th Heaven*. From then on, until now, Matt hadn't expected too much from his dad. It wasn't worth the disappointment.

Matt froze when Hulk Hooligan, Matt's thorn in the flesh, threw his leg across the aisle.

"This is a tollway, Calhan. Pay a buck to pass."

"Cal-*a*-han," Matt corrected him. "I'm not paying you, Hulk."

"Then ya ain't passin'."

Matt wasn't in the mood. "C'mon, Hulk. I need to ask your dad a question."

Hulk looked at his dad, driving the bus—presumably the *only* reason either one of them was there. His dad had a truck-driving license and Pastor Ruhlen needed a driver. It was a great way to earn a little extra cash.

"Whatcha gonna ask him?"

"None of your beeswax."

"'None of your beeswax,'" Hulk mocked.

"How's Nate?" Matt asked, changing the subject. The 200-and-some-pound bully with bleached-blond hair darkened at the mention of his little brother's name. Matt had helped his brother out a while ago, and Hulk knew he owed Matt big-time . . . though he'd never admit it.

"He's with Gramma," Hulk said. Then, "He told me to tell ya somethin'."

Matt raised his brows. "Really?"

"Yeah." He motioned for Matt to lean in. Matt did. Then: *Baaarrrrraaaaappp!!!!*

Matt recoiled at the stench of the belch. Hulk guffawed and moved his leg, letting the boys pass. Matt took the opportunity to press forward, ignoring Hulk.

Matt and Lamar made it to the front of the bus where Matt's dad, Gill's dad, Alfonzo's dad, and Pastor Ruhlen sat. Mr. Hooligan, Hulk's dad, was in the driver's seat wearing shades like an 80s rock star.

"Hey, Ace," Matt's father greeted.

"Yo!" Pastor Ruhlen said to Lamar, punching the air with his fist.

Lamar looked at Matt. Matt smiled. Matt knew that Lamar was only on the trip for his sake, to help him find out about the laptop. Lamar's father wasn't there—he couldn't be there—he'd passed away before Lamar was even born. For this trip, their youth pastor, Mick Ruhlen, was taking his place as a "stand-in" father, so Lamar could be with his friends. Pastor Ruhlen was a nice guy, and funny sometimes, but he wasn't Lamar's father, as Lamar kept reminding Matt.

"Hi," Matt said to no one in particular. "Does anyone have a map?"

"What do you need a map for?" Matt's dad wondered.

"I'm trying to figure out where we're going." It wasn't a lie.

In the driver's seat, Mr. Hooligan thumped his forefinger against his head. "I got it up here," he said gruffly.

"So no one has a map?" Matt asked.

All five men shook their heads. Matt looked at his dad for a long moment.

Lamar took a different approach. "Are we going to be stopping soon? Getting some snacks? Maybe we can buy a map."

"Dude!" Pastor Ruhlen exclaimed. "We can't stop now! The retreat's only an hour away! We gotta learn to 'rough it' startin' immediately! We are the men of the wilderness, man! Unless there's a bona fide emergency, we're sailin' on through." He winked, his orange Chia pet hair bouncing with every bump.

 Matt sighed. "Okay." He made an "oh well" face to Lamar. They trudged their way back to the rear of the bus. Halfway back, Hulk threw his leg out and Matt stumbled, hitting the ground with one knee. He glared at Hulk, but the bully just laughed.

"Enjoy your trip, Calhan?!"

As if Matt had never heard *that* one before. He noticed a six-pack of Dr. Pepper at Hulk's feet. It was jiggling with every bump, too, ready to explode. How funny would it be to open one up right in Hulk's face and soak him. He resisted that thought, however, as soon as it rose up. It wasn't the Christian thing to do. Besides, Matt preferred to live.

"No map?" Alfonzo asked when they returned.

"No map," Matt said flatly.

"Not unless we stop," Lamar added, "which they refuse to do unless there's a 'bona fide' emergency."

Gill shrugged. "So why not create a bona fide emergency?"

Matt looked at Lamar.

Lamar looked at Matt. "Don't you dare pop a tire or do something hazardous."

Matt smiled. "Not all emergencies are hazardous." He pulled out his laptop. Within 30 seconds it was ready to go. He slid his finger across the small touchpad and then tapped it, clicking the word processor icon. When the program opened he created a new document and called it "BUS RIDE." Then he cracked his knuckles and placed his fingers on the thin, black laptop's keyboard.

The air in the bus was stale. Even though it was late in the fall, it was warm outside. Southern California had a way of keeping it warm during the day. This bus was destined for Landes, Arizona, but it was going to stop first.

"How?" Gill asked, leaning into the screen.

Matt smirked. He was looking forward to this one.

> Hulk Hooligan's mouth felt like cotton.
> He reached down and grabbed a Dr. Pepper.
> He popped it open and chugged it down.
> Ahhhhhh . . . relief. Then, before he
> knew it, he had chugged down his entire
> six-pack.

Matt found the key with the clock face on it—right above the enter key. He pressed it. On screen, the cursor changed into a clock face and flashed gold, then white, then gold, then white, as it ticked forward like lightning. That's all it took. Suddenly make-believe became reality.

Gill shrugged. "I don't get it. That's not much of an emergency."

"Give it time," Matt said.

The four boys watched Hulk intently.

He yawned and smacked his lips, then looked down at his six-pack of Dr. Pepper. He pulled one out of the plastic webbing. When he opened it, it fizzed and popped and spit on his clothes. "Ugh!" he cried.

"Hey!" the kid across the aisle shouted. "Chug Challenge! 60 seconds! Go!"

Hulk, never the guy to turn down a challenge, smiled wide and began chugging. *Gulp! Gulp! Gulp! Gulp!* One! He popped open the second. It fizzed and popped and spit on his clothes. "Ugh!" *Gulp! Gulp! Gulp! Gulp!* Two!

Pop! "Ugh!" *Gulp! Gulp! Gulp! Gulp!* Three!

Pop! "Ugh!" *Gulp! Gulp! Gulp! Gulp!* Four!

Pop! "Ugh!" *Gulp! Gulp! Gulp! Gulp!* Five!

Pop! "Ugh!" *Gulp! Gulp! Gulp! Gulp!* Six!

"Stop!" the challenger cried, holding his watch.

But Hulk had already finished. He was out of Dr. P's. Kids and dads sitting around Hulk stared at him in awe. Six cans in 60 seconds. That had to be a Guinness world record.

Hulk received high fives from his companions and bragged that he could have downed another had he had one. This victory dance went on for about 10 minutes when Gill finally shrugged again. "I still don't get it, Matt," he said. "I think maybe your storytelling is a bit misguided."

Matt leaned back. "Five ... four ... three ... two ... one."

Hulk patted his stomach and then slowly stood. He stumbled to the front of the bus and said something to his dad. The five men at the front shook their heads and Hulk left the group, his shoulders hunched. He returned to his seat, appearing very uncomfortable. Then he started fidgeting and wiggling.

Gill smiled. "Matt, you are brilliant."

"I know, I know. Thank you, thank you."

A minute later, Hulk got up and walked to the front again. This time, they could hear him begging. "But I really gotta *go!*"

"Always showing off," his dad said. "Next time you'll think first."

"Sorry, Hulk," Pastor Ruhlen said. "We have to go straight through. You can hold it."

"I *can't* hold it!"

"Hold it, boy," Mr. Hooligan ordered.

> They could hear Hulk begging. "But I really gotta *go!*"

Hulk trounced back to his seat.

Matt twisted his lip. "They're not budging. Man, I thought they'd stop for sure."

"You can't just assume what's gonna happen," Lamar pointed out. "You have to think these things through. Work on your plot."

"My plot is foolproof," Matt protested. "It's just . . . missing something."

Gill laughed. "You just need to speed it up."

"What do you suggest?" Matt asked.

Gill whispered in Matt's ear.

"Okay, whatever you say."

Lamar put his face in his hands. "I can tell this is going to get hazardous," he whimpered.

Matt wrote:

> Alfonzo's dad pulled out his harmonica and began playing.

Matt hit the clock key. The on-screen cursor flashed golden and ticked forward. A moment later, Mr. Zarza pulled out his harmonica and started playing randomly.

"Hey, do you take requests?" Gill shouted.

"You know I do!" Mr. Zarza yelled from the front of the bus.

"'River of Life!'"

Alfonzo's dad started playing, and the entire bus erupted in shouting/singing the old gospel favorite:

There's a river of life flowing out of me!
Makes the lame to walk and the blind to see!
Opens prison doors, sets the captives free!
There's a river of life flowing out of me!

"No!" Hulk shouted. "Stop singing! No river!" He was squirming in his seat, trying to cross his thick legs. His face had turned red from resistance. The faces of those around him turned red, too, but from laughter.

Then the bridge:

> *Spring up o well! Within my soul!*
> *Spring up o well! And make me whole!*
> *Spring up o well! And give to me your life abundantly!*

Hulk jumped up and ran down the aisle. "STOP THE BUS! I'M GOING TO WET MY PANTS!!!"

At the very next exit, the bus took a wild turn into a Stuckey's Truck Stop. No one wanted to go river rafting *before* they made it to camp.

Matt stretched his legs and felt his back pop as he exited the bus. The QoolQuad—as Matt, Lamar, Gill, and Alfonzo called themselves—had found a dandy map at the truck stop, but it still didn't make much sense now that they had made it to their destination. They couldn't find a Rural Route 1 anywhere. Matt decided to let it rest and stuffed the map into the front pocket of his blue backpack, right under the small CD case that held the latest albums of his favorite groups: dc Talk, Relient K, and Bleach. That was another of the laptop's benefits; Matt could listen to music while "roughing it."

"Where are the showers?" Matt wondered out loud.

Pastor Ruhlen chuckled as he passed and winked at Matt. "Nature provides her own showers."

"Are you saying we wash in the river or something?" Lamar asked, following him to the back of the bus, where the luggage and tents were stowed.

Pastor Ruhlen winked again. "Bingo! I've got a smart boy with me."

"Great," Gill muttered.

Mr. Hooligan met the youth pastor at the back of the bus and unlocked a storage compartment.

"Nature provides her own showers."

He shouted for his son, and Hulk came running. "Unpack this," Mr. Hooligan ordered. Hulk didn't hesitate. He reached in and pulled out one bag after another. He started tossing them and the families separated as each boy and his dad searched for their belongings.

Matt and his dad sifted through the packs of luggage, looking for their own.

Matt stopped for a moment and turned to his dad. "It's pretty rough out here, huh?"

Mr. Calahan chuckled. "Yeah, no Playstations. It'll be nice to get away from everything, won't it?"

"I guess," Matt said. "Don't know if I can get used to washing in the river though. Won't it be cold?"

"No, it'll be *freezing*."

Matt and his dad both laughed.

"Of course," Matt said, "you're not roughing it too much—you've got your phone."

"Well, it's just for emergencies," his dad replied.

"Hope you don't get any," Matt mumbled.

At once, his dad stopped going through the bags. He straightened himself slowly, and then looked down at his belt. He unclipped the cell phone. He began to flip it around in his hand. "Have, uh ... have I been using this a lot lately?"

Matt kept rummaging through the bags. He shrugged. "I guess."

"Tell you what. This weekend, it's just you and me. No technology. Agreed?"

Matt looked up at his dad. *Was he serious? Was he about to give up his cell phone for the weekend?* Matt nodded. "Okay."

"Put it in your backpack." Matt's dad handed the phone to Matt. Suddenly the phone vibrated and Mr. Calahan pulled it back. He looked at the display. "Um ... I gotta get this, but it'll be the last time." And he walked away, speaking into the receiver.

Matt let out a short breath. He glanced over at Gill and his dad, yakking it up. He spied Lamar and Pastor Ruhlen laughing together. And there he was, on his own again. Hulk finally tossed out Matt's pack and Matt picked it up, throwing it behind him. He grabbed his tent, too, and waited for his dad's pack.

Gill and his dad came by a moment later, their gear in hand. "Hey, hey!" Gill said. "What do you think of this?" He put his right hand on his hip, his left holding his tent. He cleared his throat, then, "Carter Tents," he announced in a deep voice. "Rugged gear for the great outdoors."

Matt just looked at him.

"Was it good? I'm practicing for my commercial."

"Your commercial is for tents?"

"I have no idea what the commercial is for. But it *could* be for tents. What do you think?"

Mr. Gillespie asked, "You all right, Matt?"

Matt shook it off. "Yeah. I'm fine."

"So what do you think?" Gill pressed.

His dad grabbed him by the shoulder. "Timing, Gill," he said. "That's the first lesson for great comedians. Timing. You have to learn when it's time to have fun and when someone's not in the mood."

"Matt's always in the mood."

Mr. Gillespie glanced at Matt's dad, talking on the phone. "You think so, huh?"

"It's all right," Matt said. "It was brilliant, Gill."

"See, Dad?"

"Timing, Gill."

Alfonzo ran over with his dad, a grown-up version of his Hispanic son. They both wore forest green jackets and black jeans. "Is this the greatest or what?! This is *serious* camping!"

"Oh boy," Matt said.

And Alfonzo and his dad were off. When Lamar approached, Gill and his dad walked away. It didn't take Lamar any time to see what was bothering Matt.

"Hey," he encouraged, "we all have family challenges sometimes."

"It just never ends," Matt said, then, "Forget it. It doesn't matter. I didn't come out here because I wanted to spend time with my dad or anything." He jerked his head toward the blue backpack on his shoulder. "I came out here to get some answers. And that's exactly what I intend to do."

The Race Downstream

2

Where's the camp?" Matt asked.

They had parked the bus in a dirt parking lot, surrounded by nothing but trees of all shapes and sizes. A small wooden shack sat to the north. It was nothing more than a gigantic box with a single, wide window in the front—propped open with a stick. A muscular man with long, black hair, a red bandana, and a limp exited and made his way to Pastor Ruhlen's side.

As the fathers and sons stood waiting for instructions, Matt noticed how quiet it was in the wilderness. At home, at school, at the park, *wherever*, he was used to hearing a highway off in the distance. But not today. Today they were in the middle of nowhere.

"Pastor Ruhlen said the camp's downstream," Lamar answered Matt's question.

"We have to walk downstream?"

"No!" Alfonzo exclaimed. "We get to canoe!"

"Canoe?"

"Canoe!"

"I don't know how to canoe. Do you?"

"Can't be that hard," Lamar said. "Just paddle."

Pastor Ruhlen called the fathers and sons over. "And bring all your gear!" he added. He explained that their camp was indeed two miles downstream. He introduced limping, red bandana-man as "Pete" and said he'd start them in the right direction.

"Arrr, this is me shop," Pete grunted, pointing to the shack with his thumb.

Matt and his friends exchanged glances. Was this guy *trying* to be a pirate . . . or was he *really* a pirate? He seemed a bit over the top . . . which wasn't that surprising since he was friends with Pastor Ruhlen.

"Follow me," Pete commanded.

Following Pete the Pirate, the troops trudged past the shack and into the woods. As they entered, Matt noticed Gill closely inspecting the plant life. He was scratching his arm now, too. They followed a not-so-well-laid path, which eventually brought them to the bank of a wide stream. To Matt's left, facing downstream, was a rickety dock, lodging about 20 canoes. Each canoe appeared seaworthy enough, though the years of patches and touch-ups were evident on the wooden hulls.

Pete addressed the group. "Arrrright! Two per canoe, mates, 'n dad's in the back! Keep yer supplies within the beam, 'less ya wanna go swimmin'. Everybody enters port side, and be sure ta enter and exit low. Keeps ya stable. Watch the thwart and the ribs—ye amateurs always're trippin' over 'em." He held up a stained life jacket in one hand and a discolored helmet in the other. "Everyone wears a PFD and a helmet—no exceptions, got it? If ya capsize, stay with yer canoe."

Capsize? Matt thought. *Does he mean tip over?* Matt adjusted his backpack on his shoulder. There was no way he could allow his laptop to get wet.

"I've scouted the river and ya should be fine all the way down ta camp. Mick can lead ya. Just stay low and stay in the light water." Pete pointed downstream. "When ya break into the river, you'll see dark water on the starboard side. It's deep and it's fast and ya don't need ta be near it. Any questions?"

Gill raised his hand. "Where's your parrot?"

Pete scowled and didn't bother answering him.

"Great," Lamar whispered, "just tick off the pirate, why don't ya?"

"What?"

Gill's dad grabbed him by the neck. "Timing."

"All right!" Pastor Ruhlen addressed everyone. "This will be a good opportunity to learn to work together. Paddling isn't easy, dudes. It takes teamwork and lotsa concentration. No goofing around. But you can do it. And remember: last one to the campsite is a rotten egg roll!"

Cheers emerged from the crowd.

Lamar whispered to Matt, "No using your laptop."

"Who, me?"

Two by two, Pete the Pirate and Pastor Ruhlen helped the boys and their dads gear up and enter their canoes with their belongings. Matt's dad had rejoined them during the lineup and now shoved his phone in Matt's backpack after turning it off. "All done," he said simply.

Matt forced a smile.

Finally, when everyone was sitting in the stream, Pastor Ruhlen and Lamar entered their own canoe and paddled to the front of the group. Pastor Ruhlen shouted for everyone to follow him, and take it easy. Pete waved good-bye.

Like a row of cars merging onto a highway, the fathers and sons moved down the stream single file until they finally broke out into a wide river.

When they hit the waterway, Matt let out an embarrassing yelp as the current jarred their canoe.

"It's all right," his dad said, sitting behind him. "Row the direct opposite of me. Starboard side, then port side. I'll row port, then starboard."

Matt peered over his shoulder at his dad. "Which side's port?"

Mr. Calahan smiled. "Left."

"Right."

Port, starboard, port, starboard, Matt began to paddle. The boat rocked as their oars licked the water. Each time Matt lifted up his oar and swung it to the other side of the boat, river water sprayed him in the face.

"Smoothly," Matt's dad said.

As Matt pulled his oar through the water, he felt his left arm already beginning to ache. He pulled the paddle back with a jerk and soaked his jean shorts. The water was freezing. Matt had shoved his backpack into a cubbyhole in the front of the canoe. He watched the water piling up in the center of the boat and worried that it might run down and soak his backpack.

"Careful, don't fall behind me," his dad said.

Matt grimaced. He pushed harder.

Alfonzo and his dad zipped past them like Olympic race contestants. Alfonzo asked if they could go in the darker water and really pick up speed.

"Patience," his dad said. "Practice makes perfect."

Matt and his dad continued to row sporadically. Matt tightened his jaw as he pressed ahead. Suddenly, they passed the Gillespies.

"Hey!" Gill shouted. He started throwing water at Matt with his oar. Matt's dad splashed him back, giving him a flood in the face. "Augh!"

Matt laughed. "Go, Dad!"

Up ahead, Hulk and his father were arguing about who should guide the canoe. Matt and his dad sailed past them as if they were standing still. Of course, they pretty much were. Matt smiled broadly, and didn't mind if Hulk noticed.

"We rock!" Matt said to his dad.

"Yeah, we're not doing too bad—but don't get over confident. To really get going we have to work together like Alfonzo and his dad . . . especially if we want to make it *upstream* at the end of the trip."

"Yeah, I know." Matt didn't even want to *think* about going upstream. Downstream hurt enough!

"Let's take a break. Save our energy."

Matt happily agreed. He pulled his oar up and balanced it on the ridge of the boat. For the first time since they entered the river, he stopped to look 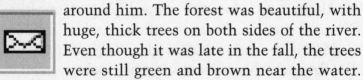 around him. The forest was beautiful, with huge, thick trees on both sides of the river. Even though it was late in the fall, the trees were still green and brown near the water. He could hear birds and crickets and snaps of twigs. Matt closed his eyes for a moment. He took a breath of fresh, cool air and imagined that "roughing it" may not be so rough after all. With such peaceful sur-roundings and his dad's phone zipped away, what could possibly go wrong?

Then suddenly, a shiver crawled down his spine and the hairs on the back of his neck stood straight up. He opened his eyes. He had the eerie notion someone was watching them. He had the feeling they weren't alone.

Matt jumped when a flock of birds burst out of a tree across the river . . . as if something . . . or some-one . . . had disturbed them. He reached down to his feet and picked up his backpack. He threw it over his right shoulder, feeling the weight of his laptop hit his back. *Better to be safe than sorry.* He was about to say something to his dad when *Slam!*

"*Oooof!!*"

Hulk and his dad rammed the Calahan's canoe, knocking Matt forward. Matt caught himself, but his oar flew away from him. He lurched out to grab it when his backpack slipped off his shoulder and shot down his arm. He gasped and twisted around to catch it—and then he lost his balance.

For a split second, Matt felt himself teetering on the edge of the canoe, and then he knew he was going over, as gravity pulled him down. "Matt!" Mr. Calahan cried as he swung forward and grabbed onto Matt's arm while trying to steady the canoe. Matt felt the water pulling him under while his friends and their fathers began to shout. Matt lifted his backpack above him as he went under. He immediately bobbed back to the surface, pulled up by his life jacket. His jaw clasped as the frigid water soaked him to the bone. With his dad holding his left arm, it was all he could do to keep his backpack out of the water with his right. The bottom had already become wet and all he could think about was his laptop.

"Don't let go!" he cried to his dad.

"Don't let go of the backpack!" his dad said. "My phone's in there!"

"Your phone?! My laptop's in there!"

"You brought your laptop camping?"

"You brought your *phone!*"

Matt's dad kicked the canoe around as best he could as Mr. Hooligan blamed his son for the accident. Matt didn't know if he'd hit them on purpose or not, but Hulk was wearing a smirk.

"You okay?" Hulk's dad asked.

"Yeah," Matt mumbled.

Matt grabbed the side of his canoe and his dad let go of him. Mr. Calahan snatched the backpack from Matt, unzipped the front pocket, and pulled out his cell phone. He flipped it open. He shook it. He pushed the buttons. "Great," he said. "It's dead."

"How's my laptop?" Matt asked.

"You'll have to check it out later."

Pastor Ruhlen and Lamar pulled up on the other side of Matt and the youth pastor grabbed Matt's belt at his back, and shoved him back into his canoe.

"I'm sorry about your phone," Matt said ... though he wondered if now his dad would give up his work for the weekend.

"You shouldn't have had your backpack on your shoulder. Why didn't you leave it in the front of the boat?"

Matt shrugged.

The other canoes pulled away, and the teams continued downstream.

After a long moment, between paddles, Matt's dad asked, "You really brought your laptop?"

"You brought your phone."

Mr. Calahan huffed and then said, "Well, I'm glad you're all right. You scared me. If we don't pay attention and work together, Matt, this is the kind of trouble that can happen."

Matt looked at the bottom of his backpack. Sopping wet. *Trouble was right.*

Their campsite was a small clearing, just off the left bank of the river. When they arrived, Pastor Ruhlen advised everyone to exit the canoes before they bottomed out on the rocky riverbed. Soaking their feet in the river, everyone followed his instructions. Jumping into the water was fine with Matt; he was already wet. The teams lifted the canoes and walked them onto land.

As soon as they were safely ashore, they all removed their helmets and life jackets and got to work. One tent after another popped up around the perimeter of the campsite. In the center, a wide circle of logs was arranged around a circle of rocks with ashes in the middle. Matt and his dad picked a random spot and threw their stuff on the ground.

Matt unzipped his backpack and pulled out his laptop. His dad sat on a nearby tree trunk and started messing with his phone again. Matt inspected his machine and smiled. The laptop had been sitting on top of an extra pair of jeans—and was completely dry. *Thank God*.

Then Matt remembered the map. He caught his breath; he had stuffed it into the bottom of the backpack's front pocket, underneath his CD case. Matt dug into the pocket and pulled out the CD case first—it was drenched—and then the map. It fell limp in his hands. When Mr. Calahan saw Matt pull it out, he shook his head—one of those "told you so" kind of headshakes. Matt found a small, clear area nearby, where he lay down his map and carefully unfolded it. It would dry and Matt and his friends could find out exactly where they were going.

"Well, we'd better get started." Mr. Calahan clipped his dead phone to his belt.

Matt ignored him. Whenever his dad got in a mood, Matt just ignored him. It wasn't his fault that the phone was fried. Well, okay, maybe he shouldn't have put his backpack on his shoulder, but even his dad wasn't prepared for Hulk to slam into their boat. It was Hulk's fault, clear and simple. If his dad couldn't accept that ... well, then maybe he deserved a ruined phone.

Matt and his dad measured out where to place the stakes. Then they spread their tent out and prepared to raise it. Mr. Calahan showed Matt how to drive the stakes into the ground with the wire attached for firm grounding. Matt looked at their tent, spread out like a bedsheet, and he sighed. This was going to take *forever*. Why couldn't Matt and his dad have one of those really cool tents that "popped" into place with a flick of the wrist? Instead, they were stuck with a two-person tent with wires and stakes and bars and rods.

As Matt tied a wire to a stake and pulled it taut, he looked over and saw Gill and his dad laughing. Alfonzo and his dad were already setting up the interior of their tent. Matt stomped the stake into the soil as hard as he could.

Lamar, raising his tent with Pastor Ruhlen, looked like he was enjoying himself about as much as Matt. Sometimes when it came to doing "guy stuff," Lamar got frustrated. Without a dad around, he felt like there were a lot of things he'd never learned how to do. Matt understood. Maybe that's part of the reason they were best friends.

Hulk ran past Matt, a Nerf football in his hands. "I'll call you onto my team if we get too far ahead!" he razzed Matt.

"Heh-heh," Matt pretended to laugh. He glanced over at Mr. Hooligan, Hulk's dad, on the other side of the camp, putting up his tent alone. Matt wasn't sure if he wanted to do it alone or if Hulk just wouldn't help.

"Hey, Matt," Mr. Calahan said. "You go ahead and play football with the guys. I can get the tent."

Matt looked at his dad. He wondered if that was a nice way of saying, "I'd rather do it alone."

Matt stood and grabbed his backpack. He threw it over his shoulder. "K." As he glanced back and saw his dad raising the tent alone, it made Matt wonder again why they were there in the first place.

Matt looked over at the map, drying behind his tent. And he remembered exactly why he was there. He was there to find a clue and get one step closer to solving the mystery surrounding his laptop.

Bonfire Blues

3

Let's sing 'River of Life'!"

Hulk threw Gill a disapproving look. "Shuddup."

Pastor Ruhlen smiled. "Stay cool, comrades! How 'bout we sing this one?" He started strumming a song on his guitar that they'd learned in youth group. As they recognized it, everyone joined in.

The fathers and sons were all sitting on logs around a blazing campfire, in the center of their camp. Surrounding them were 12 tents, all surprisingly dark and small within the forest cove. Each father sat by his son. Lamar sat by Pastor Ruhlen, who was strumming away like a rock-star wanna-be, while Alfonzo's dad, once he "felt out" the chords, joined in with his harmonica.

Just an hour before, they had eaten hot dogs and beef jerky and drank blue Kool-Aid for dinner. It looked to Matt like this would be their sustenance for the next few days. Of course, that wasn't a bad thing, so long as no one asked what was in the hot dogs, or why the Kool-Aid was blue.

Matt was still steaming. If it wasn't bad enough that his dad had blamed him for ruining his phone, when Matt returned to his tent after football, his map was gone. When he asked his dad what happened to it, he just said, "Who cares? We're here to 'rough it,' Matt, remember?" That really irked him. What right did his dad have to throw away his personal stuff? It wasn't as if he was a kid anymore. He was thirteen. And that meant something, didn't it?

A few songs later Pastor Ruhlen started a game of Operator. He whispered a "secret phrase" into Lamar's ear, and Lamar whispered it into Alfonzo's dad's ear. The whispering continued around the circle until Matt's dad whispered it in Matt's ear and Matt announced what the "secret phrase" was: "The baby's tooth hated two groups of punch."

Pastor Ruhlen then told them the real "secret phrase": "Babe Ruth ate Froot Loops for lunch."

Then there was, "Don't play hopscotch on the stairs." This ended up as, "Don't way upchuck or you'll get stares."

And finally, Matt couldn't figure out how "Rocket science isn't for rocket scientists" turned into "Socket wrenches taste better with elephant wings." Nonetheless, it got the biggest laugh of all.

As the laughter died down, Pastor Ruhlen put up a hand. "Dudes! Listen up! There's a valuable truth to be learned." He opened his Bible and thumbed through it. "Communication," he emphasized, "is very important between fathers and sons. And it doesn't always have to be deep. Many times, just being there for each other is enough. In fact, being there is what fathers and sons are all about."

> **"Communication is very important between fathers and sons."**

Matt's dad nudged him. "Hey, Ace, you still upset?" he whispered.

"It's not my fault your phone got ruined," Matt shot back.

Mr. Calahan let out a long breath. "I know. I was just frustrated. I'm sorry. I just needed it in case there was a work emergency."

"Dad, you get work emergencies all the time."

"Well ... Matt ... I'm working for you and your mom. We couldn't live in such a nice house and you couldn't have stuff like your laptop if I didn't work."

Matt crossed his arms in front of him.

Pastor Ruhlen continued, "Now, check out this verse, dudes; I love this verse. John 5:20: 'For the Father loves the Son and shows him all he does.' Wow! God showed Jesus what he did. He trained him. God is setting the example for us. He wants fathers and sons to communicate. He wants sons to learn from their fathers. But wait! There's more. This verse goes on to say, 'Yes, to your amazement he will show him even greater things than these.' Did you get that, dudes? God not only taught Jesus, but he showed him greater things all the time. He set the example of *mentoring*. He set the example of a father training a son in the secrets of life."

"Why'd you have to take away my map?" Matt demanded in a hushed voice.

"Matt, is that what you're upset about? You know you don't need a map out here."

"But that doesn't mean you can take it. You don't know how important it was for me to have that map."

"You know what?" Mr. Calahan continued. "I didn't take your map. I don't know who did. Maybe it blew away, but I didn't take it."

"Right."

"Why are you so upset, Matt?" his dad asked. "What else can I say?"

Matt wanted to burst out with *I don't care about having a nice house and laptops and stuff! When was* 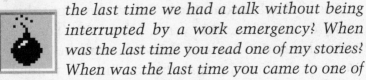 *the last time we had a talk without being interrupted by a work emergency? When was the last time you read one of my stories? When was the last time you came to one of my games and paid attention?* Instead, he just huffed.

"I can't believe you're just upset about the map. You know what I think? I think you're hiding something, Ace. And I'll tell you something else—if you've got a secret, I'm going to figure it out."

Matt's head snapped to his dad. *Was he serious?* Matt felt his stomach turn. He couldn't let his dad know about the laptop. He and Lamar and Gill and Alfonzo had agreed to keep the laptop a secret no matter what. They knew they *had* to keep it a secret—even from those they loved most. On one hand, they couldn't tell anyone because it was just too powerful of a secret. Everything they had typed in the laptop so far had actually happened—exactly as they typed it. And if that kind of power fell into the wrong hands ... well, the thought made Matt shiver. On the other hand, Matt and his friends were aware that just *knowing* about their secret brought the possibility of danger. And they didn't want to force danger on anyone. So, the four boys had agreed that they couldn't tell anyone about the laptop. No matter what.

> **They knew they *had* to keep it a secret.**

"I think," Pastor Ruhlen was saying, "the hardest thing for a father to do is *be* a father. Many dads just want to be best friends with their kids. But you guys have best friends. You need a dad. Someone to 'bring you up in the training and instruction of the

Lord,' like Ephesians 6 says. A mentor. Someone to help you through these teenage years. Young dudes, your dad can be your mentor if you'll let him. You can learn a lot from him. And dads, believe it or not, your sons *want* to learn from you."

Matt glanced at his dad. He had never thought of him as much of a mentor. He only thought of him as a dad. Matt wondered what he could learn from him . . . other than Answering Phones 101.

"In the Bible, you can see that Samuel had Eli as a mentor. Timothy had Paul. And, of course, as we see here, Jesus had Father God. That's part of the 2:52 principal—He grew smarter, stronger, deeper, and cooler 'cuz of his relationship with his Dad. Remember Luke 2:52?"

Heads bobbed up and down around the campfire.

Pastor Ruhlen quickly added, "The Big Guy Upstairs places men in our lives to advance us in our calling. And those truths you learn from your mentor happen through the years, through spending time together. The secrets of life are always revealed in time. And even if you don't have a father at home," he concluded, giving Lamar a wink, "if you have someone who can be a mentor, you're not alone." He asked everyone to bow his head as he prayed. Then, after the prayer, he shouted, "How 'bout some S'mores?!"

Cheers shot up around the circle, and before long, the boys and their dads were mashing roasted marshmallows between graham crackers and Hershey's chocolate.

Mr. Calahan was carefully constructing his first S'more when he sat down beside Matt, who was already on his second. Matt wasn't sure about what to say, and his dad was quiet, too. His father put his S'more in his mouth and then about spit it on the ground as it burned his tongue. Matt let out a laugh. Mr. Calahan started joining in, but then stopped and said, "So . . . you forgive me?"

Matt opened his mouth to answer when Gill appeared, holding something in his hands.

"Look what I found!"

Matt backed away. "Is that a Pooka Dooka?"

Mr. Calahan excused himself, saying he needed some cold water.

"Pooka Dookas are supa-dupa!" Gill said in his best advertising voice—sounding just like the commercial for the animal cookies stuffed with bright green goo.

Matt grimaced. "No, they're not! They're gross!"

Gill laughed and tossed the Pooka Dooka into the bonfire. It fizzled when it hit.

"Who brought those?" Matt asked.

"Hulk!"

"You're kidding me?! Hulk likes Pooka Dookas?"

"I guess. Someone needs to tell him Pooka Dookas make-a you puke-a!" he quipped. That's what Gill always said about the gross-tasting cookies.

"Seriously. Hey, you gotta tell Lamar."

"Where is he?"

Matt looked around the camp. He saw his dad talking to Alfonzo's dad and Gill's dad. Pastor Ruhlen was talking to some kids Matt barely knew. Then Matt spotted Lamar all by himself, walking toward the river, kicking a rock.

"Hey, I'll be right back," he said to Gill.

Matt jogged over to Lamar, slowing down the closer he came to his friend.

"Hey, Lamar, Gill found some Pooka Dookas."

Lamar shook his head quickly and sniffed, stopping his walk. He managed a weak smile. "Tell him to save me one."

"Gill said they make-a him puke-a."

"Yeah."

The company back at the camp sounded distant now, like when someone threw a party at the end of Matt's block. He could hear them and see them having fun, but it was almost like watching a TV show.

Matt turned back to Lamar. He shifted his backpack. "So . . . is this the way to the bathroom?"

"You came out here to ask me where the bathroom was?"

"Well, when you gotta go, you gotta go."

"The bathroom is all around you. They're called trees."

"Right. But I mean the real bathroom. Didn't someone say there was a brick outhouse or something around here? Maybe your dad knows."

"Pastor Ruhlen knows," Lamar said sharply, "but he isn't my dad."

Matt heard a sound and turned. Alfonzo was heading their way.

"I know," Matt said. "But still . . . he's pretty cool."

> "The bathroom is all around you. They're called trees."

"Whatever."

"You don't like him?"

"You don't understand, Matt."

Alfonzo nodded as he met Matt and Lamar. "I understand," he said.

"*You* understand?" Lamar asked Alfonzo. "You of all people don't understand. You and your dad are, like, perfect."

"What's wrong with Pastor Ruhlen?"

"Nothing. It's just . . . not the same."

"No, it's better."

"*How* could it be better?"

Alfonzo stepped forward with an intense look in his eye. "It's better because you have a mom *and* a dad. My mom left us—just left us. Left Papa, Isabel, me—alone. Pastor Ruhlen says you're not alone because you got him. And you got your mom. Iz and me and Papa—we know what it's like to be alone. Mom left and we're alone."

"Well, it's not easy for me either," Matt shifted on his feet. "I have a mom and dad, but half the time I'm on hold. 'Matt, hold on! Gotta get this!'"

Lamar and Alfonzo stared at Matt, who suddenly saw how weak his point was. He continued, "I mean, I don't know what either of you are complaining about. It could be worse. We *could* all have dads like Hulk who practically don't even acknowledge us."

Lamar and Alfonzo continued to stare at Matt.

"What?"

They continued to stare.

Matt said, "Hulk's behind me, isn't he?"

The boys nodded. Matt turned and saw Hulk storming away. *Great.*

Lamar brushed by Matt. "I'm going to bed."

Alfonzo brushed by Matt and said, "Me, too."

"Fine!" Matt shouted. "I'm going to . . . the bathroom!"

"Fine!" Lamar shouted back.

Matt stormed off toward the woods. What was everyone so upset about? It wasn't a perfect world. *None* of them had it perfect.

Everything seemed different since his thirteenth birthday. His mom had entered the room with a single cupcake and a trick candle. His dad had worn that goofy smile. He wished he could freeze time and keep from blowing out that candle. If only things didn't have to change so much, so fast. Life used to make sense. Now he and his best friends were fighting about stupid stuff. Now he and his parents couldn't get their timing right. Whenever they wanted to spend time with Matt, he wanted to be alone. But when he wanted to do something with one of them, business always interfered. The laptop didn't make things easier either. His dad always talked about getting gray hair because of stress; Matt wouldn't be at all surprised to wake up one morning to find a lock of his hair turning gray from stress just like that X-men character Lamar sometimes drew. And if that wasn't enough, Matt still couldn't figure out why he could barely put a sentence together around Alfonzo's sister, Isabel. *Well,* he relented, *I'm kind of looking forward to whatever it might take to fix that problem.*

He thought about Isabel for a moment and warmed. He thought about her straight, midnight black hair that tumbled

He thought about Isabel for a moment and warmed.

down her back like a waterfall. He thought about her innocent, 12-year-old, deep brown eyes that took in everything. He thought about her voice that dripped like newly spun honey. He thought about the fact that she was staying at his house with his mom while they were on their father/son retreat. He thought about his mom, who was probably even now sitting down and showing her his baby pictures . . . especially her favorite ones where he had the chicken pox. *Great.*

Matt stopped at the edge of the woods and looked around to make sure no one was near. He guessed he'd really have to go to the bathroom the old-fashioned way. How embarrassing.

He couldn't see a thing. He squinted into the dark 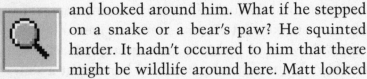 and looked around him. What if he stepped on a snake or a bear's paw? He squinted harder. It hadn't occurred to him that there might be wildlife around here. Matt looked back toward the camp. Maybe he shouldn't be so far away.

He slid his backpack off his shoulder and pulled out his laptop. He popped it open and pushed the power button. As the machine booted up, the Wordtronix logo spun around and the screen shone brightly. Matt smiled. He turned the laptop around and aimed it toward the ground in front of him. The screen cast a blue glow on the earth. He'd just dare a snake to try to hide now!

Matt took a few steps into the edge of the forest. He heard a hundred crickets singing from all directions.

He stopped when his foot hit a twig. He moved the laptop down to light the ground.

And he froze.

A sudden shiver crawled down his spine.

A gasp escaped his parted lips.

His eyes grew wide in surprise.

Suddenly he realized his dad was telling the truth; he wasn't the one who had taken his map.

For there, carved in the mud, was a single word that haunted Matt to the core of his being. Someone had scrawled:

WORDTRONIX

4

Caught in the Current

'm telling you," Matt emphasized, "it was written right here last night."

Lamar studied the ground and finally stood. "Well, there's nothing there now."

"Who would have written that?" Alfonzo asked.

"I, for one, don't want to know," Gill admitted, scratching his leg.

Matt had barely slept a wink all night after seeing the message. His friends—especially Gill—had barely slept either.

After spying the cryptic message in the mud, Matt had returned to camp to tell Lamar, Gill, and Alfonzo about it. Though no one was in a very good mood after their spat, hostilities quickly vanished when the threat of danger became evident. Since the laptop's power was a secret between the boys—a secret they vowed to never reveal—they decided to keep the mud message a secret, too. Regardless, each of the boys found it a little easier to relax during the night with their dads/youth pastor in the same tent.

Gill pulled a stick of beef jerky out of his pocket and started chewing.

"Where'd you get that?" Lamar asked.

Gill reached in his pocket and pulled out about 25 sticks. "At the campfire last night. Want some?"

"No . . . thanks," Lamar said. "You know, only truck drivers eat beef jerky."

"I think that's a semi-truth," Gill quipped

"Let's get back to camp," Matt suggested. For all he knew, the trees had ears.

The boys started back, and then suddenly they heard a rustling behind them. They stopped. The rustling stopped. They started moving again. The rustling started again. They stopped again.

"Who's there?" Alfonzo said boldly.

"Please promise you won't kill me," Gill interjected.

"Who's there?" Alfonzo demanded again.

And suddenly, something burst through the bushes like a wrecking ball through an old building. "BOOO!!"

> And suddenly, something burst through the bushes like a wrecking ball through an old building. "BOOO!!"

"Aughhhhhhhhh!" everyone cried. Alfonzo and Lamar stumbled back. Gill dropped his jerky. Matt whirled around and ran into a tree.

Matt was about to run when he heard Lamar accuse, "Hulk!"

"I knew it was you," Gill said to Hulk, brushing off his jerky.

"Me too," Matt said, rubbing his forehead.

"What are you doing here?" Lamar asked.

"What're *you* guys doin' here?"

"You have to answer our question first."

"I'm following ya."

"Why?"

"Because yer all actin' *stupid* ... not dat dat's unusual ... "

"We were just heading back to camp," Matt said.

"Me too," Hulk said, blowing it off. "Goin' ta see my dad who don't even acknowledge my existence."

"Hey," Matt said, running in front of him. "I'm sorry I said that, Hulk. You know I didn't mean it."

"Whatever, Calhan!" he said, pushing Matt out of his way. "Ya think just 'cuz ya tutored me and helped out Nate dat ya own me. Lemme tell ya somethin'. No one owns me—especially a football flop nerd like you."

Hulk stomped away, shaking the earth like a tyrannosaurus rex.

"I knew it was just him in the bushes," Gill repeated, scratching his leg again.

Matt rolled his eyes. "Gill, stop scratching," he said sharply. "You don't have poison ivy."

"I know! My leg just itches."

"Whatever." His friends followed him back to camp.

After a short way, Alfonzo said, "We've been here a full day now and the only thing we've done is set up tents. I need some adventure."

"We're practicing our canoeing this afternoon," Lamar reminded him.

"Yeah, canoeing where I can't go in the fast water. I know. C'mon, when are we going to find the house?"

At the edge of the camp, Matt said, "I thought you said you couldn't care less about finding the house. You said you just came for fun."

"Yeah, but I'm not having fun—no one will let me. I need *extreme* adventure. And if I don't get any, I'm going to play football with Hulk."

"Hulk?!" Matt protested. "He just called us football flop nerds!"

"No, he just called *you* a football flop nerd."

"Thanks."

"Well," Lamar said, "I don't know if we should try and find the house anyway. This is getting dangerous. A stolen map. A message in the mud. It's creeping me out."

"Finally! Someone with sense!" Gill cried.

Matt turned and kept walking. "Well, I still want to find it. I want answers. This is our only chance.

I'm not saying we need to put ourselves in danger . . . but I think we owe it to ourselves to at least get a glimpse of Rural Route 1, Box 87."

"So . . . when do we start?" Alfonzo urged.

"A writer needs time to plot his story."

"What is there to plot?" Alfonzo asked.

"Matt's got a point," Lamar noted. "We need to take time to plot this story or we'll end up with a situation like what happened in the bus. It almost didn't work out."

"It *did* work out though," Gill noted.

Matt protested. "Yeah, but a plot gives us substance. Lets us know the *exact* direction we want to go. A clear goal helps you fill in the blanks when you write. Good plotting takes time, patience, blood, sweat, and tears."

"Well, we've got a clear goal!" Alfonzo countered. "We want to find the house."

"Right—but *how* do we want to find it? Like— oh, never mind." Now in the camp area, Matt stopped and sat down on a log. He pulled his laptop out of his backpack. Lamar, Gill, and Alfonzo exchanged glances as it booted up. Then Matt wrote:

```
The band of four cool guys, the QoolQuad,
found the exact address they were searching
for: RR1, Box 87, in Landes, Arizona.
```

Matt hit the clock key and the on-screen icon flashed golden, the clock face ticking forward quickly.

"That's it?" Lamar asked.

"That's what I was trying to tell you," Matt said. "If I don't have time to plot, this is the sort of drudge you end up with. It's not a story, it's just a sentence."

"Actually, it's not that bad," Gill complimented. "It's got a subject and a verb. The *perfect* sentence."

"Well, at least we know we'll find the place when we start looking," Lamar pointed out. "So when do you want to start, Matt?"

"I'll let you know when I've worked out the plot," Matt said.

"Ugh!" Alfonzo exclaimed. "I'm going to play football with Hulk."

Around the bend from the camp was the entrance to the lake, where all 20 canoes had found their home on the shore. After practicing on the lake for nearly an hour, Matt and his dad still couldn't find their rhythm. One or the other was going too slow or too fast. Matt found it hard to concentrate. Matt and his dad had been nice enough to each other the past 12 hours, but they hadn't really said much. Matt felt awkward; he didn't know exactly what to say. His dad must have shared his feelings because he kept the subject to things like paddling and lunch food. Matt felt a bit silly, too; he'd blamed his dad for taking his map . . . and he most likely *hadn't* taken it.

Then, out of the blue, a funny thing happened: Mr. Calahan's cell phone started working again, ringing like an alarm clock. Of course, that wasn't the *funniest* thing. The *funniest* thing was when Matt's dad ripped it off his belt, shouted, "Hey! It works!" and then pitched it thirty yards, over the water and onto the land. It skidded to a stop in the mud.

Matt about choked. "Dad!" he cried. "Your phone!"

Mr. Calahan didn't even flinch. "Told you, I don't need it. If you and I are gonna be a team this trip, we don't need my business interrupting."

Matt picked his jaw up off his feet and started laughing. "Dad, that was seriously *awesome!*"

"I can be seriously awesome sometimes," Mr. Calahan said, nodding.

> **Matt didn't know what to say. His dad was actually being cool.**

Pastor Ruhlen called everyone in to shore to get ready for dinner. "Hot doggers and Kool-Aid!" he announced.

The father/son teams paddled to shore and exited their canoes. Matt was still stunned that his dad just launched his cell phone. As they drew into land, Matt didn't know what to say. His dad was actually being cool.

"Hey, Pop!" Alfonzo called to his dad. "You mind if I stay out here and practice a little more?"

Mr. Zarza shrugged and caught Pastor Ruhlen's eye. "Okay by you?"

"Fine by me," the youth pastor said as the rest of the troops pulled in.

Then Mr. Calahan did another cool thing. He said, "Hey, you wanna stay, too? I'll go help with lunch. Just keep your life jacket and helmet on and stay safe."

"Dad, are you feeling all right? Maybe you've caught Gill's poison ivy."

Mr. Calahan laughed. "I was up late last night. Made some decisions. Things are going to be different. I promise."

Lamar and Gill quickly got permission, too, and the fathers were happy, given the safety in numbers. Hulk just told his dad he was going to stay, and his dad shrugged and walked away.

When Matt's dad climbed out of the canoe, he reached for Matt's backpack in the front. Matt had wrapped a life jacket around it, knotting it tight, to keep it safe. Matt blocked his reach.

"C'mon," his dad said, "I'll hold it for you. It'll be safer on the shore with me."

Matt thought about it. "Um ... but I don't think ... "

"Really, Matt. You don't want it to get wet, do you?"

"No, but I just ... " Matt looked at Lamar for a quick answer, but Lamar just shrugged.

Mr. Calahan looked at the backpack then back at his son. For a second, Matt lost his breath. What was he thinking? Mr. Calahan stood back and put up his hands. "Okay, whatever you want, Matt. I don't want to start a fight."

Matt watched his dad walk back down the path to camp. As he passed his grounded cell phone, he reached down, picked it up, and dusted it off. Matt shook his head. He knew he couldn't get rid of it. He might be dramatic with it, but he wouldn't get rid of it.

"Your laptop might be safer with your dad," Lamar whispered to Matt.

Matt let out a long breath. "I guess. But if *they* are out here looking for it ... I don't want to hand it to them gift wrapped with a bow on top."

Alfonzo broke the tension by splashing the water with his oar. "Okay, let's team up. Who's with me?"

"Me, totally!" Gill exclaimed.

The boys managed to put two of their four canoes back on the shoreline. The other two stayed in the water. Matt and Lamar manned one boat, Gill and Alfonzo manned a second. Hulk parted from the QoolQuad and manned his own boat.

"You gonna be all right going alone?" Alfonzo asked Hulk.

The big guy spat in the water. "I'm my own team," Hulk explained. "I don't need any of ya to weaken me."

Alfonzo looked at his friends with big eyes and they all chuckled.

Each team kicked out into the river and paddled.

Matt could already feel the rhythm of each paddle. He asked Lamar, "How come we can stay in sync, but me and my dad are like a clown act?"

"Probably," Lamar suggested, "because we're both doing it wrong."

As the three teams made their way upstream, Matt's arms quickly tired. Paddling against the current was extremely difficult. He wondered how he and his dad would ever make it back to Pete the Pirate's. The boys crawled several lengths up and then swirled their canoes around. As they paddled backward to keep from being carried forward by the current, Matt and Lamar looked at their competition.

"Ready?" Alfonzo asked.

"I was *born* ready," Matt responded.

"You're TOAST!" Gill shouted and dug his paddle into the water. At once, the three teams were off. They shot forward, downstream, racing neck and neck. Matt and Lamar tried to get a rhythm down by

chanting the guard march from *The Wizard of Oz.*
Gill and Alfonzo just shouted, "Go! Go! Go! Go!"
with each paddle. Hulk *was* his own team, already
passing them both.

Matt's oar hit Gill's and his friend accused him of
trying to thwart the race. Matt laughed and plunged
forward. With each row, water splashed them,
drenching them from head to toe. Matt got more wet
from Lamar's rowing than from his own.

Suddenly, Gill and Alfonzo's canoe sharply veered
away from Matt and Lamar.

"Yaaahhh!!!" Gill cried. "What are you doing?!"

"We're gonna beat Hulk!" Alfonzo announced.

"Faster!" Matt shouted back at Lamar.

"Where are we racing to?" Lamar asked.

"The third tree leaning in the water!" Alfonzo
shouted. "And *we're* getting there *first!*"

"In yer dreams!" Hulk shot back.

Matt and Lamar pushed forward as Gill and
Alfonzo veered farther. Suddenly . . .

Gill and Alfonzo's canoe hit deeper water and the current sped up. Gill screamed.

"We're going too far!" Gill
shouted.

"We're going *faster!*" Alfonzo
insisted.

"Too fast! I can't—"

Whoosh! At once, Gill and
Alfonzo's canoe hit deeper water

and the current sped up. Gill screamed—he actually *screamed*—when his oar flew out of his hand. Gill and Alfonzo's canoe shot forward, passing Matt and Lamar as if they were standing still.

Hulk groaned when Gill and Alfonzo flew past him, too.

"We win!" Alfonzo shouted as they passed the third tree.

"Aw, man!" Matt huffed.

Alfonzo dug into the current with his oar in an attempt to pull them back onto course. The canoe suddenly whipped completely around and the boys were flying backward down the river.

"Aaaaaauuuggghhhhhhh!!!" Gill screamed again.

Alfonzo panicked. "I can't control it!"

"We're out of control!" Gill added. "We're gonna die! Help!"

Matt reached for his backpack, ready to pull out his laptop—when he suddenly realized Hulk was staring right at them. He looked back at Lamar, who was biting his lip, looking at Gill and Alfonzo.

"C'mon!" Matt said, paddling on the right, pulling him and Lamar into deeper water.

"Hold on!" Lamar shouted to Gill and Alfonzo.

"We're gonna die!" Gill shouted again. "Matt, I leave my stereo to you!"

"We're coming!" Matt cried.

"You're crazy!" Hulk shouted, crashing into the tree. "You're crazy!"

"Matt!" Lamar cried. "You're paddling the wrong way! Teamwork, man! Teamwork!"

"I'm not paddling wrong, you are!"

"I am not!"

"Are too!"

"You're crazy!" Hulk shouted, his canoe wedged between two thick branches. He couldn't get free.

Whoosh! Matt and Lamar hit the current and fell in right behind Gill and Alfonzo. The two canoes zipped downstream like NASCAR race cars on their final lap. Hulk's shouts suddenly became distant as they left him far behind.

> **The two canoes zipped downstream like NASCAR racecars on their final lap.**

Smack! Lamar's oar caught a rock and it yanked out of his hand.

Matt's eye caught the terrain— one stream flowing into another, speeding them up at every pass. "We're gonna get lost!" Matt shouted.

"We're gonna die!" Gill replied.

"Stop saying that! We're not gonna die!" Alfonzo pulled against the current with his oar.

Whap! At once, Matt's canoe hit a large rock and nearly capsized.

"Teamwork, Matt!" Lamar shouted louder.

Matt thought about reaching for his laptop, but there wasn't time to untie it from the life jacket, take it out of the backpack, boot it up, and use it.

Whump! The two teams dropped five feet over a small waterfall. Again, they nearly tipped.

Whump! Whump! Whump! Whump! Down, down, down, down, farther they fell as they joined another river.

"Matt!!!" Alfonzo shouted, pointing to the next waterfall. "Big one ahead! Use the laptop!"

"I don't have time!"

Alfonzo's head whipped around and Matt saw the panic in his eyes.

"We're gonna die!" Gill repeated.

"We *are* gonna die!" Alfonzo agreed.

"I don't wanna die!" Lamar insisted.

"We're *not* gonna die!" Matt pressed.

He jabbed his oar forward and caught the end of Gill and Alfonzo's canoe. Lamar leaned forward and the two boys pulled tightly to bring the boats together. But instead, it jerked Gill and Alfonzo's boat left, flipped it onto its side, and dumped the boys out. Gill grabbed onto Alfonzo and Alfonzo grabbed onto Lamar's oar. Upside down, Gill and Alfonzo's canoe roared downstream, flew over the big waterfall, and was gone.

The four boys were carried a short way until Matt and Lamar's canoe hit another large, sharp rock and split in half like an egg. Matt, Lamar, and Matt's backpack spilled into the water like yolks into a frying pan. Like trying to save a baby, Matt instinctively grabbed his backpack and popped it above his head, letting his life jacket do its work on him. Matt could barely see as the river splashed him in the face.

The four boys, popping up and out of the water like bobbers, latched onto one another for safety. The current shoved them downstream like driftwood.

Matt braced himself.

Lamar braced himself.

Gill braced himself.

Alfonzo braced himself.

The roaring of the river filled their ears. And they all knew that, in a second, they were going over the "big one."

5

Lost

"Heeeeeeeeeellllllllllllllp!"

One! Two! Three! Four! The QoolQuad dropped over the waterfall, plummeting into the water below like misfired cannonballs. Their life jackets popped them to the surface. Matt gurgled for air as he splashed through the water surrounding him, grasping for something, anything, that he could latch onto.

"Matt!" he heard Lamar cry.

Matt kicked forward, shaking the flood out of his mind. "Lamar!"

"Your laptop!"

Matt spun around, still moving quickly down the river, caught by the current. His laptop, inside his backpack, wrapped in a life jacket, was floating away quickly. Suddenly a hand grabbed him.

"Gotcha!" Lamar bellowed.

Matt grabbed Lamar's arm and saw that his friend had caught Gill, too. He pulled Matt aside and nodded to the large log he was lodged against. On the other side of him, Gill pulled himself to shore.

"Follow him," Lamar ordered.

Matt gladly obeyed.

"Where's Alfonzo?!" he cried.

Lamar nodded downstream. Alfonzo was running along the shoreline, following the laptop. When he was significantly ahead, he darted out onto an old log and waited for the laptop to come to him. When it did, he snatched it out of the water like a pelican grabbing dinner.

"Got it!" he shouted.

Matt let out a sigh of relief.

All four boys finally collapsed on the riverbank and tried to regain control of their breathing. Matt untied the life jacket from the backpack and took out his laptop. It was slightly wet, but when Matt pressed the power button, it fired up like a champion. Matt gave his friends the thumbs-up.

"I think I'm unconscious," Gill said.

Matt glanced at him. "You're what?"

"I'm unconscious."

"Gill, if you were unconscious, you wouldn't be talking."

"Oh, good! Then I'm alive. Is my face okay for the camera?"

Lamar shook his head. "Sorry, man. It looks the same as it always has."

Matt chuckled. Lamar and Alfonzo chuckled. Gill

promised Lamar he'd forget him when he was rich and famous.

Gill's Idea

A half hour later, Matt finally stood. He stared at the raging waterfall, the waving trees, and then the tranquil sky.

"Where are we?" Lamar wondered, standing beside Matt.

"I have no idea."

"We need to contact our dads," Alfonzo noted. He pushed himself up.

"How?" Matt asked. "We're in the middle of nowhere. The Internet probably doesn't even exist out here."

"Use your laptop."

Matt mumbled something about poor plotting. Then he booted up his laptop once again and launched the word processor. He cracked his knuckles and wrote:

```
The four castaways had taken off on a
three-hour tour, but were exhausted and
ready to get back to camp. They found
their way easily, using their many years
of wit and wisdom.
```

When Matt pressed the clock key, the golden icon flashed on-screen, ticking forward.

For a full minute, the QoolQuad stood still, waiting for something to happen.

"So what do we do?" Lamar asked finally.

"We head back, using our many years of wit and wisdom," Matt said.

Each of the boys looked at each other.

"So what do we do?" Lamar repeated.

"Any suggestions?" Matt asked.

Gill hopped up. "We can send smoke signals!"

"We can *what?*"

"Yeah, I saw it on *The Lone Ranger.*"

"The who what?" Lamar asked.

"The Lone Ranger."

Matt, Lamar, and Alfonzo drew blanks.

"The cowboy show where the masked hero always says, 'Hi-Ho, Silver! Away!'"

"We have no idea what you're talking about," Lamar said dryly.

"You're kidding me? It's a fifties TV show. My dad has it on DVD."

The boys all shrugged.

"Anyway, in this one show, Tonto gets lost and—"

"Tonto?"

"Sidekick Indian."

"People actually watched this show?"

"Tonto gets lost and builds a fire. He uses the smoke to make signals and call for help."

The four boys stood silent for a moment.

"Why don't we just walk back?" Matt finally suggested.

Lamar and Alfonzo nodded.

"Sorry," Lamar apologized, patting Gill on the shoulder. "Don't mean to dis Toto."

"Tonto," Gill corrected. "Toto's a dog."

They started walking, but then Gill stopped them in their tracks. "Wait! What if we're being hunted?!"

"Hunted?" Lamar repeated.

"Hunted! What if they're tracking us?!"

"Who?"

"Them!" Gill said. "The crazy Wordtronix people that we were warned about!"

Matt shook his head. "We don't have to worry about *them*, Gill. We don't even know where we are. I'm sure they don't either."

They started walking again when Gill stopped in his tracks once more. "Wait! What if we starve before we get back to camp?!"

"Starve?" Lamar asked.

"Starve! What if our bodies can't take the trek?"

Matt clutched Gill's jacket. "Is this the same jacket you were wearing this morning?"

"Yeah."

Matt put his hand in Gill's front pocket. He pulled out a fistful of beef jerky. "We'll be fine."

"Yeah," Alfonzo said. "And I have cookies."

That got Matt, Lamar, and Gill's attention. "Really?" they all asked in unison.

"Yeah. From Iz." He pulled one out of his pocket. It was safe inside a small, airtight baggie. "She made one for each of us. I was going to give them to you guys at lunch."

"Cool."

"*Way* cool."

Once again, the boys started walking.

Matt's Idea

"So if we don't use smoke signals, how exactly are we going to find the camp?" Gill asked.

"We'll just follow the river," Matt reasoned.

Gill shrugged. "Oh, okay."

The QoolQuad made their way up the side of the steep ledge, listening to the raging waterfall as they climbed. When they reached the top, they each stared at the river ahead of them. It forked in two directions.

"Which one did we come down?" Matt asked.

"The right one," Lamar said. "Definitely."

"Actually," Alfonzo stated, "I think it was the left one."

Gill shrugged. "Maybe we should split up."

"We're not splitting up," Matt said.

"They always split up in the movies."

"They never split up when it's too dangerous. And it's too dangerous now."

"They *always* split up when it's too dangerous."

Matt pointed to the right fork. "I think it was the right one, too. Let's take it. We can always come back."

The boys agreed and moved forward. Fifteen minutes later, they came to another fork—this time with three branches flowing into one. They looked at each other for a long moment until Gill left the group and started picking up twigs.

"What are you doing?" Matt asked.

"I'm building a fire. Toto and I have decided to send smoke signals."

Alfonzo's Idea

Alfonzo said, "I learned once that moss grows on the north side of trees. We came in from the south. So if we follow the moss on the trees, it should take us back to camp."

Gill stood with a batch of twigs in his hand. "And you guys think *smoke signals* are a bad idea?"

"It's worth a shot," Lamar said.

"Let's go," Matt agreed.

They made their way into the forest and started checking out trees until they found one with olive green moss growing on it.

"This way," Alfonzo pointed.

They continued forward, turning occasionally to set themselves in the right direction.

"I know we're getting closer," Matt said at each turn. "The laptop wouldn't lead us wrong."

After nearly four hours of walking through the forest and shallow riverbeds, the boys froze in their tracks.

"Footprints!" Alfonzo spied.

Matt bent down and studied them. "Tennis shoes. We must be close to *someone*."

"Thank God!" Gill cried, chewing on a stick of beef jerky. "I'm starving!"

They walked a few feet forward and stopped in their tracks once more.

> **They were close. They could *feel* it.**

"More footprints!" Alfonzo spied again.

Matt bent down and studied them once more. "More tennis shoes."

They walked farther until Alfonzo spotted another set—and then another.

"I can taste the hot dogs now!" Gill said emphatically.

They jogged forward, getting more excited by the moment. Gill shouted out his dad's name, eagerly hoping for an answer. They could *feel* it. They were close.

Suddenly, Alfonzo stopped in his tracks.

"What?" Matt asked, kneeling beside Alfonzo. "More footprints?"

"Not exactly."

"Then what?" Gill wondered.

"Gill, what's the brand of your beef jerky?"

"I don't know," he said, pulling out a stick and studying its plastic wrap. Then, in his best advertising voice, he said, "They're Big Jim's Beef Jerky. Don't be jerky. Eat beef." He laughed. "Want one?"

"No thanks," Alfonzo answered. "I'll just take *this one.*" He stood, pinching a stick of Big Jim's beef jerky between his fingertips.

"Cool!" Gill shouted. "We must be *really* close!"

"I don't think so," Matt said, disappointed.

"What do you mean?"

"I think this is some beef jerky *you* dropped. An hour ago."

"What's it doing here?" Gill asked.

"These are *our* footprints," Lamar stated flatly. "We're going in circles."

"But the moss . . . it . . . "

"Apparently grows on the north, south, east, *and* west sides of trees," Alfonzo admitted.

Lamar's Idea

Matt ran his hand through his hair. "You guys, we're *lost.* Admit it. Our dads are probably freaking."

"They know we can take care of ourselves," Alfonzo said, "as long as we put our heads together."

"Yeah, we're doing a great job so far," Gill said, rolling his eyes.

"We really need to pray," Lamar suggested.

> "God, we're really lost. We need your help."

Matt let out a long sigh. "You're right. We should have done that earlier."

Lamar nodded. "C'mon, hand stack."

The four boys put their hands atop one another, in the center of their circle.

"God, we're really lost," Lamar began. "We need your help. Give us wisdom, we pray, to know where to go. Help the guys at camp to find us. Guide us, we pray. In Jesus' Name, amen."

"Amen," the boys agreed. They raised their heads . . . everyone except Alfonzo.

"What?" Matt asked.

Alfonzo bent down. "There's another set of footprints here."

"What?" Matt, Lamar, and Gill bent down, too.

"Here," Alfonzo said, tracing the oblong print. "It looks like a . . . cowboy boot."

The boys looked at each other's shoes.

"None of us are wearing cowboy boots," Lamar whispered.

"Then who left this?" Alfonzo asked.

"The Lone Ranger?" Gill suggested.

Matt gulped. "Is *anyone* at camp wearing boots?"

His three friends shook their heads. Suddenly a twig snapped in the distance, and the four boys jumped up at once.

Gill whispered, "If this footprint isn't from anyone we know ... then," he gulped, " ... *who's* that?"

"If I had to guess," Matt answered, "I'd say it's ... *them.*"

The Laptop Did It ...
Again

6

Ruuuuuuuuunnnnnnnnn!!!!!!"

Matt, Lamar, Gill, and Alfonzo ran through the forest as fast as they could. They ran farther and farther, retreating deeper and deeper—anything to get away from whoever was obviously on their tracks.

Matt felt his breath giving out with each stomp. More than once a branch smacked him in the head or the chest, burning as it slapped. He kept looking back, trying to see if he could catch a glimpse of *them*. Alfonzo didn't look back once.

Matt's heart pounded like a bongo drum inside his chest. As his legs became numb, he slowed. He jumped a small stream, and then looked back. He didn't see anything menacing. No hunter, no ogre, no wild animal. Just the quiet forest. Finally, Matt stopped.

Lamar halted with him and Gill stopped a moment later. Far ahead, Alfonzo beckoned them to catch up with him.

"C'mon!" he yelled.

Matt was busy gasping for air.

"You think ... he's still following us?" Gill asked, breathing heavily.

Lamar shook his head. "I think ... we lost him."

Alfonzo kept waving, but they ignored him.

"Where does he get his energy?" Matt wondered.

Then suddenly Alfonzo sunk into the ground.

Matt blinked.

"What?" Lamar stared at the spot where Alfonzo had been and dropped his jaw.

"Where'd he go?" Gill asked. "Alfonzo!"

Matt slapped Gill on the chest. "Don't yell! You want the Lone Ranger to find us?"

"I'll never watch that show again," Gill promised.

The three boys jogged ahead to where Alfonzo had stood only moments before. It was growing darker, especially in the thick areas of the forest where the evening sun couldn't penetrate.

"Whoa!" Lamar cried and grabbed Matt's arm just in time.

Matt looked down to see the edge of a short cliff. About 15 feet down, Alfonzo was waving to them.

"Guys, get down here!" he encouraged. "You're not gonna believe what I found!"

The QoolQuad scratched their heads as they stood at the cave entrance Alfonzo had discovered between two sharp drops in the land. It was a small entrance, maybe seven feet tall, and it was boarded up like the windows on Alfonzo's house before he had moved in.

"What is it?" Matt wondered. "An old mine?"

"Maybe they mined gold here," Lamar suggested.

That got Gill's attention. "Gold?! You think there's any left?"

"If there were, do you think they'd have stopped mining?" Matt asked.

Gill shrugged. "Maybe they ran out of money."

"If you're finding gold, you don't run out of money."

"Who cares what it was?" Lamar said, looking up at the sky. "It's getting dark and we need a safe place to stay for the night. Then we can get a fresh start tomorrow."

"I don't understand," Matt admitted. "The laptop has never failed us. Why can't we find our camp?"

"Maybe the water shorted it out," Gill submitted.

Alfonzo found a weak spot in the wood and with a *SNAP!* and a *CRACK!* he pulled a plank off. The entire structure creaked like an old door opening. He stuck his head through the decaying boards. "¡Hola!" his voice echoed inside. He *SNAP!-CRACK!ed* two more boards off—just enough to slide through, but not to make it noticeable to anyone passing by. Better, Alfonzo said, not to give *them* any clues.

He motioned to the others. "Who's first?"

Gill looked at Lamar. Lamar looked at Matt. Matt looked at Alfonzo.

Alfonzo shrugged. "Okay, I guess me."

Alfonzo threw one of the broken boards into the cave and listened for any peculiar sounds. When none came, he picked up the other broken board and held it tightly. Then he stuck one foot through the small entrance he had created and slithered the rest of his body into the cave. Matt, Lamar, and Gill peered in, trying to see what he was doing.

"What do you see?" Matt asked.

"Is it full of rattlesnakes with poison dripping from their fangs?" Gill asked.

Matt and Lamar looked at Gill.

"Thanks for that visual," Matt said.

"I can't see much of anything," Alfonzo 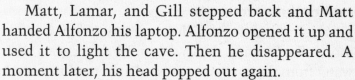 replied. "You guys are blocking my light."

Matt, Lamar, and Gill stepped back and Matt handed Alfonzo his laptop. Alfonzo opened it up and used it to light the cave. Then he disappeared. A moment later, his head popped out again.

"It's safe," he said. "There's nothing in here. I can't tell how far back it goes, but we should be safe for the night."

"What if our dads come looking for us?" Gill asked.

"We should be able to hear them," Lamar pointed out, "as well as . . . anyone else who might be looking for us."

"I'd better not die," Gill stated. "Can you imagine what would happen to me if I died before becoming famous?"

Matt guessed, "You'd be posthumously famous?"

"Your writer's vocabulary leaves me speechless."

"You can look it up when we get home," Matt said. Then, "You're not going to die. I don't know why you've got that on your brain."

"Well, what about water? We can't live without water. We could die of thirst!"

Alfonzo slipped back through the broken cave entrance and joined his friends outside. He reached into his jacket pocket and pulled out a stack of cookies, each one individually wrapped inside a plastic baggie. Each sugar cookie had one of the boy's names on it, etched in smooth, pink frosting. He handed each cookie to its owner.

"Here," he offered. "These are the cookies Iz made for us. Eat 'em and then we can fill the baggies with water from the stream we crossed a short while back."

"But it's getting dark!"

"You and I'll go together," Lamar assured Gill. "C'mon. Eat your cookie before it gets any darker."

Matt and Alfonzo handed their bags to Lamar and Gill who climbed back up the hill, eating their cookies.

Matt turned his sugar cookie around in his hand. Etched in the pink icing, Matt's sweet snack said:

Matt— ☺

Matt smiled. If he weren't so hungry, he wouldn't have eaten it. He would have encased it in Plexiglas. It was really nice of Alfonzo's sister, Isabel, to make them cookies. Matt's smiley face looked like it was winking at him. His heart swelled.

Fifteen minutes later, the four boys all sat safely inside the dank and dark cave, eating beef jerky and drinking mossy-tasting water from Ziploc bags. They could just barely see each other as their eyes adjusted. Their only light shone through the sliver of an opening Alfonzo had created in the boarded-up entrance. Matt and his friends shivered as the evening brought in cooler weather.

"This is so boring, just sitting around and waiting 'til morning," Alfonzo said, gnawing on a stick of beef jerky.

"You think our dads are looking for us?" Gill wondered.

"Are you kidding?!" Matt tossed back. "They've probably already called in the SWAT team. Well, at the very least, they're running through the forest with flashlights like the government guys in *E.T.*"

Gill stuck a crooked finger in Matt's face. "Beee gooooood," he said in a raspy voice.

Matt pushed Gill's finger away from his face.

Lamar nudged Matt. "Hey, why don't you tell us a story? You've always got a good one up your sleeve."

Matt thought about it a moment, and then, "We just shipwrecked ourselves in the wilderness, got chased by a mysterious hunter in cowboy boots, and now we're holed up in an old, abandoned mineshaft. I can't beat that."

"I could practice my commercial!" Gill offered. He held up a stick of beef jerky. "Big Jim's Beef Jerky," he said in a thick, Western accent, "fresh from the best Western cattle! Now they're on sale for only 50 cents a stick, so get ready for the bargain stampede of the century! Yee-haw!"

"Hi-ho Silver!" Alfonzo interjected.

Matt shook his head. "Bargain stampede? What's *that* all about?"

Gill shrugged and chuckled. He scratched his leg and leaned in for a closer look. "Guys, my leg keeps itching! You think maybe I did get poison ivy?"

"You're imagining things," Lamar said.

"How in the world did we get here? We could be around a campfire right now instead of shivering in this cave."

"How in the world did we get here?" Alfonzo asked. "We could be around a campfire right now instead of shivering in this cave."

"I don't know," Gill blurted. "Maybe it had something to do with you trying to navigate the fast part of the river before we were ready."

"Hey," Alfonzo retorted, "I could have handled it, but my shipmate picked the wrong time to freak out on me."

"Don't lay into Gill for this," Matt said. "He's not the one who went off into the deep end."

"I didn't go off the deep end."

"I said *into* the deep end."

"What's the difference?"

"The word 'into.'"

"Guys, chill," Lamar said. "None of us did the right thing."

"I tried to save their lives!" Matt protested.

"We were working too much against each other to help them," Lamar stated.

"Well, since when have you not wanted to do things by yourself?"

"Hey, this isn't my fault. Alfonzo's the one who went off the deep end!"

"*Into* the deep end!" Alfonzo snapped. Then, cooling down, he added, "Okay ... maybe I did go a little *off* the deep end."

Gill looked up. "Hey, no. You're right. My timing was all messed up. That's what my dad's been trying to tell me."

"It doesn't matter," Matt interjected. "Lamar's right. If I had tried to work with Lamar instead of against him, we might have been able to save you guys."

"No, really," Lamar said, "I know I haven't been myself lately. There was no way for you to know it was any different."

There was a long silence until Alfonzo repeated, "So how in the world did we get here? We could be by the campfire instead of shivering in this cave."

"Good question," Gill answered. "Guess we're not the perfect 2:52 sons."

Lamar shrugged. "Hey, you know what Pastor Ruhlen says: 2:52 is about us growing smarter, stronger, deeper, and cooler—not about being perfect."

"You're saying I'm not perfect?" Gill kidded.

Matt decided to change the subject. "Those were good cookies."

"Iz makes great desserts," Alfonzo noted.

Matt glanced at Gill. "So . . . did she spell your name correctly?"

"Yep. But it's not hard to remember the name of a famous redhead."

"Yeah," Matt said coolly. "And then she put a winky face after your name, huh?"

"A what?"

"A winky face. On your cookie."

Gill glanced at Lamar. "You mean a smiley face? I had a smiley face. What's a winky face?"

"Same thing as a smiley face, but winking."

"I think you misread it," Lamar said. "Mine was definitely a smiley face."

"Mine too," Alfonzo said.

"Yeah, mine too, probably." Matt smiled to himself on the inside. He got a winky face. His friends only got smiley faces. Too bad for them.

"Man, you should have had her make more," Lamar joked. "Good stuff."

> "Hey, you know what Pastor Ruhlen says: 2:52 is about us growing smarter, stronger, deeper, and cooler—not about being perfect."

"She's just like Mom," Alfonzo said in a somber tone. "Mom taught her."

Matt was glad it was dark. He knew the subject of his mom pained Alfonzo. He rarely mentioned his mom, but from what Matt gathered, his parents had divorced just before his dad transferred to his job in the States. Apparently, his mom just up and left one day, leaving only a nasty note on the kitchen table. Matt couldn't imagine ever finding a note like that.

"I don't think I'm too much like either one of my parents," Matt said, trying to release the tension.

"Are you kidding?" Lamar piped up. "You're exactly like your dad."

Matt was taken aback. "My dad? Okay, you're kidding, aren't you? Half the time he's lost in his work."

"Yeah, like you get lost in your laptop."

"I what?"

"Matt, when you start writing, you get lost in your work, too. I mean, look at you. I can tell: The thought of losing your laptop has had you up in arms the whole trip."

Matt shifted. "Yeah, but writing's important. A writer can change the world. A writer can change 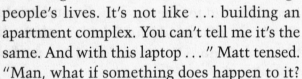 people's lives. It's not like . . . building an apartment complex. You can't tell me it's the same. And with this laptop . . . " Matt tensed. "Man, what if something does happen to it? I lose a whole lot more than my writing."

"I rest my case."

"What?"

"I *know* I'm like my papa," Alfonzo stated matter-of-factly, turning back to the subject at hand. "We like *all* the same things. Everything we do is the same. Lots of people say we even look the same."

Matt thought. "You do look the same."

Lamar let out a slow breath. "I wonder how much I'm like my dad." He shrugged. "I know I look like him a little bit. We have the same brown eyes. Same forehead, my mom says, but I don't see it." He took in a deep breath. "You know though, as much as I hate to admit it, it is kinda cool having Pastor Ruhlen on this trip with me. I had to give him a chance, but he's pretty decent. You know we even stayed up half the night talking about art and stuff? You know he reads half the comics I like to draw?"

"Dude!" Matt quipped, just as Pastor Ruhlen always did. The boys laughed.

"Yeah, that's why I say you gotta give your dad another chance," Lamar said. "I mean, you can learn something from him, can't you?"

Matt drew a circle on the floor with his finger. "Well, he's been trying to teach me about teamwork."

"Yeah, he's not so bad. You ever talk to him about your writing? I bet he'd like your stories."

"I don't know if I'd ever show him one of my stories," Matt said. "He'd probably get a phone call halfway through reading it."

"Man, if his phone calls bother you that much, why don't you say something?"

Matt shrugged. "It doesn't matter. Besides, I don't think he'd get my stories anyway."

"Well, you should say *something*," Lamar pressed.

"Sometimes I don't wanna be like my dad," Alfonzo said.

"Why not?" Matt asked.

Alfonzo shrugged. After a short pause, he added, "I know Mama doesn't like him any more. She said so."

"Man, c'mon," Lamar said, "your mom isn't gonna think any less of you if you're like him."

"It's bad," Alfonzo said. "You don't know how bad it is. It's *bad.*"

Gill spoke up. "My mom was married once before she met my dad."

"Still," Alfonzo said. "Your parents are together. It's different."

"Actually, I don't know about my birth parents," Gill corrected him. "I'm adopted."

"Seriously?"

"Yep."

"Wow. I guess I'm not surprised, you being from Mars and all."

Gill pushed Alfonzo. "Well, I'm adopted, but my parents *feel* like my birth parents. I call them my parents. Don't know if I'll ever know my real birth parents."

"Don't you want to?"

"I don't know. I guess."

"You know what's weird?" Lamar said. "Thinking that my mom might start dating. She brought that up the other day."

"She brought it up?" Matt asked. "You think she wants to go out with someone?"

Lamar shrugged. "I don't know. I hope not. I don't think I want her to date."

"Maybe she could marry Pastor Ruhlen," Matt suggested.

At the same time, all four boys shouted, "Dude!" The boys laughed.

Then Alfonzo said, "Hey, all this stuff ... don't tell anyone."

Matt thought about these secrets ... somehow becoming a teenager had brought so many secrets into his life. He didn't have a clue as to why. His mind jumped to the secret he was holding: his laptop ... and the mysterious message left on the Internet by Sam Dunaway at RR1, Box 87. "If you've come here, then I must be dead and you must have the Wordtronix." Had he received the laptop because Sam's secret had been revealed? Had Sam lost his secret to a hunter in cowboy boots ... a hunter that was still out to find the laptop?

He shivered and put his hand in the center of their circle. Lamar, Gill, and Alfonzo stacked their hands on his. "Team," they said together.

Then Matt added, "Some secrets are meant to stay that way. And if they're not, maybe Pastor Ruhlen's right. Maybe they'll be revealed soon enough."

Tick ... tick ... tick. Lamar's watch woke Matt up the next morning before anyone else. He had used his backpack as a pillow all night, so he knew his laptop was safe. The sun hit his eyes and he stumbled toward the cave entrance and squeezed between the planks. The morning air in the mountains was cool and crisp, like the feeling you get when you break a leaf off a head of lettuce. Well, that's the first thing Matt thought of anyway. He stretched, yawned, and looked around. He walked a little way and peered at the treetops peeking over the opposite, sharp hill. Suddenly one caught his eye. But it wasn't a treetop. It was ... the sharp point of a housetop.

Matt climbed the hill, opposite the one they'd climbed down the day before. At the top, he looked down and saw a small, fragile-looking cabin in the wilderness. But what caught Matt's eye wasn't the oddity of a dwelling in the wild.

What caught Matt's eye was the mailbox in front of the house, at the end of a long, narrow, and twisted dirt drive. Displayed across the mailbox's side, just below a rusted red flag, were clear block letters:

RR1
#87

The laptop had done it again—made the future happen just as Matt had typed it. The band of four cool guys, the QoolQuad, had found the exact address they were searching for ... whether they really wanted to or not. The laptop wasn't malfunctioning. It was just performing one command before another.

Pursued and Trapped

7

Can I just say that laptop is amazing?" Lamar said.

"You got that right," Gill said with a gulp. "You think you could use it to help me in my commercial?" He scratched his arm.

Matt scratched his own arm. Lamar scratched his chest. Alfonzo scratched his leg. The fake poison ivy was spreading.

Matt, Lamar, Gill, and Alfonzo stood outside the small cabin in the wilderness, beside the mailbox, and stared at the front door.

"I just don't believe it," Alfonzo said, wide-eyed. "So I guess your plot was good enough after all."

Matt turned to Alfonzo. "Hardly! This is what happens when a writer isn't given time to plot. The story takes random—sometimes dangerous—turns."

"I have no idea what you're talking about."

"What I'm talking about is the fact that if *I'd* plotted this story, I wouldn't have had us plummeting over a waterfall," Matt huffed. "I wouldn't have had

us running from the Lone Ranger, or left us with
nothing but beef jerky and Ziploc-bagged water."

"Oh well," Lamar said. "It worked out."

"So what do we do now?" Alfonzo asked.

"I don't know," Matt admitted. "I guess
we knock."

No one moved.

"So who's gonna knock?" Alfonzo asked.

"I don't know," Matt said. "Who wants to go
first?"

Still, no one moved.

"I bet no one's home," Lamar wagered.

"Why's that?" Matt asked, watching the cabin.

"'Cuz in the movies, whenever the private eye
finds the house he's looking for, no one's ever home.
He has to break in."

"We're not breaking in," Matt stated flatly.

"I *know* we're not breaking in," Lamar shot back.
"None of us are private eyes."

"I could be a private eye." Gill opened the mailbox and bent down to peer inside.

"What are you doing?!" Matt cried.

"I'm looking for clues."

"It's *illegal* to open another person's mail, Gill."

"I'm not opening their mail. I'm opening their
mailbox." He closed the mailbox.

"Well?" Lamar asked.

"What?"

"What's inside?"

"You sure you want to know?"

"Why wouldn't I want to know?"

"Because Matt says it's illegal."

Lamar pushed Gill out of the way and opened the mailbox. He gasped.

Lamar pushed Gill out of the way and opened the mailbox. He gasped.

"What?!" Matt cried.

"This thing is *filthy!*" Lamar stepped aside.

The mailbox was empty.

Matt let out a long breath. "Okay. Someone needs to go knock."

"What good is knocking going to do?" Alfonzo asked. "If this is Sam's place and Sam is dead, who's going to answer?"

"Maybe Sam had a wife," Matt suggested, "or a dog."

"Here goes nothing," Lamar said.

As if their feet were connected, the boys slowly approached the house. They made their way up two rickety front steps to the front door. Matt braced himself and then, his stomach in knots, he knocked.

And they waited.

And they waited.

And they began to feel a bit foolish.

"I told you no one would be home," Lamar pointed out.

Alfonzo slid over a foot and peered into a window to the right of the door. He licked his palm and then rubbed dirt off the window. Cupping a hand above his eyebrows, he pressed his face to the glass.

"What do you see?" Matt asked.

"A table and chairs. A few clocks and paintings. A fireplace. Nothing groundbreaking, except the dust is a mile high. Old Sam must've lived alone. Doesn't look like anyone has been around for a while."

Matt twisted his lip. "There's got to be a clue here. We're missing something." He put his hand on the doorknob.

"Wait!" Gill shouted. "This is where I draw the line. If we go inside, we're breaking and entering. If I go to jail, I'll be a Hollywood scandal before even getting there! This could ruin my career!"

Matt twisted the doorknob and pushed. The door was dead bolted.

"Guess I just saved your career," he said to Gill with a wink. "C'mon. Let's check around the rest of the cabin and see if we can find anything."

The QoolQuad swung around the left side of the cabin first, but didn't see anything remarkable, save a bad fire ant problem. When they made it to the back, they found three more windows—all drawn shut from the inside with thick, navy blue and burgundy plaid curtains.

Matt thought it odd that the house had no back door. The second side to the little square structure was as unremarkable as the first—it was so disappointing. There was only a large stack of dry logs propped against the side of the cabin. He sat down on a log and shook his head.

"What?" Lamar asked, sitting on another log.

"Well, I was just thinking," Matt said. "Some things here don't add up."

"Like what?"

"Like . . . where are the phone lines to this place? The electricity lines?"

Lamar shrugged. "Maybe they use batteries and cell phones."

"They could be underground," Alfonzo guessed. "Or maybe they use solar power."

The boys looked up, but didn't see anything atop the triangular-shaped roof. Matt couldn't shake the feeling that they were just missing *something*. It was the same feeling he sometimes had in Math class when he finished a problem, but it just seemed too easy. He always wondered if he'd forgotten to carry a one or something. Matt drummed his fingers against the log . . . and then the answer hit him.

"Alfonzo—didn't you say there was a fireplace?"

Alfonzo nodded.

"So, where's the chimney?"

The QoolQuad looked at the roof again.

"My uncle has a gas fireplace with no chimney," Gill said. "He can turn it on and off with a garage door opener. It's so cool."

"Yeah," Matt said, "but if this place uses gas, why are we sitting here on stacks of firewood?"

The four boys looked at each other for a long moment. Clear that no one had an answer, Matt said, "Let's take another peek in the front window."

The QoolQuad hopped up and ran around to the front of the house, nearly tripping over each other, fighting to be the first one there.

Matt pressed ahead and hopped up the porch in one leap. He pressed his face against the window. Inside he saw the fireplace just as Alfonzo had described it. It was made from large stones, with a mantel halfway up, completely empty, save a small clock.

"Hey guys!" Matt shouted, looking around the room. "I think we're on to something! I mean, what's a stone fireplace doing inside a house without a chimney?! I don't know what it means, but it is a clue, *isn't it?*"

No one said anything.

"Isn't it?" Matt repeated.

Still, no one said anything.

"Guys?" Matt turned to look at his friends.

They were all standing there, at the bottom of the steps, staring forward, speechless.

"What?"

Gill gulped loud enough for everyone to hear.

Then Matt realized they weren't looking at him but at the window. Matt turned and looked at it again, but this time he stepped back . . . and he saw it.

In the window, above Alfonzo's fresh, clear spot, was a fresher series of clear spots . . . letters . . . written in the grime . . . spelling out the word:

WORDTRONIX

Matt felt his knees turn to jelly and his body begin to shake. "Th-th-th-that wasn't here b-b-before . . . was it?"

They shook their heads.

"Oh no."

In the silence, the boys heard footsteps . . . coming from the other side of the house.

"Go! Go! Go!" Matt ordered in a harsh whisper. "Back to the cave! Before he sees us!"

At once, the QoolQuad shot away from the cabin and over the cliff. They scaled it in half the time it took them before. They dropped to the bottom of the area between the cliffs and squeezed through the broken board entrance. They blindly ran into the back of the cave, hitting the dark cavern walls several times. At last, they froze and listened. It was so quiet, they only heard Lamar's watch *tick . . . tick . . . tick*.

"You've got to get rid of your watch," Matt whispered to Lamar.

"I'm not wearing a watch," Lamar returned.

Tick . . . tick . . . tick.

Matt felt a chill crawl down his spine. "Then whose watch is it?"

"*I'm* not wearing a watch either," Alfonzo stated.

"Mine's digital," Gill said.

Matt nodded. "Mine too."

Tick . . . tick . . . tick.

SNAP! CRACK! One of the boards at the front of the cave was ripped clean from its place.

Gill nearly screamed, but covered his mouth just in time.

SNAP! CRACK! Another board was torn away. A third board was grabbed by a big, burly hand that pulled at it, breaking apart the rusty nails.

"We're trapped!" Gill cried too loudly.

"Shhhhh!" Matt, Lamar, and Alfonzo hushed him.

SNAP! CRACK! The third board gave way. They could see a huge, dark figure looming outside. The figure grabbed yet another board.

"Go!" Matt ordered. "Deeper into the cave!"

SNAP! CRACK! **One of the boards at the front of the cave was ripped clean from its place.**

The boys felt their way deeper into the cave. They could still hear the boards snapping away as their captor drew closer to gaining entrance.

Suddenly Matt realized the ticking was louder.

Tick . . . tick . . . tick.

"Where's that ticking coming from?" Matt demanded.

"Over here!" came Alfonzo's voice.

"Where are you?"

"Over here!"

Tick . . . tick . . . tick. SNAP! CRACK!

Matt, Lamar, and Gill followed Alfonzo's voice. They ran right into him.

"Down here!" he said.

Matt bent down and could hear the ticking louder than ever.

Tick! Tick! Tick!

He felt the ground. It was no longer dirt. It was some sort of—

Tick!
Tick!
Tick!

"It's a grate!" Lamar realized.

SNAP! CRACK! At the other end of the cave, another board gave way . . . and then footsteps. Echoing footsteps.

"We're gonna die!" Gill whimpered.

"Pull it up!" Matt pressed.

All fingers shot into the grate and pulled. It wouldn't budge.

"I feel a latch underneath!" Lamar said and popped it.

As the boys lifted, the weighty steel gave way. The heavy footsteps wandered around the cave as the boys pulled the grate aside.

"I feel a ladder!" Alfonzo exclaimed in a whisper. "I'm going down!" A few seconds passed. "I'm in! I'm just going to keep going! C'mon!"

"Don't give us a play-by-play!" Lamar said. "Just go!"

Lamar jumped in next, then Gill.

Matt heard the footsteps drawing closer . . .

Matt felt Gill's head drop down. Matt slipped into the hole right behind him, grabbing onto the ladder. It was cold and rough. As he slid inside, he pulled the grate over his head, hiding them under the cave floor. He felt for the hook and latched it shut.

Suddenly the grate creaked as a foot landed on it. Matt froze. The figure above him growled under his breath. Matt shook until his teeth chattered. The figure continued on his way, apparently unaware the boys were right beneath him. They waited a long moment until the footsteps disappeared in the same direction from which they came.

"Hey, there's another grate down here!" Alfonzo announced.

"At the bottom?" Matt asked.

"Yeah! I can feel the latch with my hand. It—"

Whump!

It was the sound of a grate flying open . . .

"Augh!"

And Alfonzo falling.

8

The Secret Bunker

Help!"

Matt looked down, but it was pitch-black in the hole. "Alfonzo!"

"I'm all right," came the reply. "But I'm dangling from the end of the ladder!"

"Can you see what's below you?"

Alfonzo grunted. "Not really. But there's some sort of glow ... "

"Can you see a floor?"

"I can't tell. I think so. I don't know. Maybe."

"How far down is it?"

A few moments passed, "Maybe fifteen feet."

"What do we do?" Lamar asked.

"We're going to die," Gill shared.

"We're *not* going to die," Matt replied. "But we don't have much of a choice. We can't go up. It's too dangerous with the Lone Ranger up there. We need to go down."

"How?" Alfonzo asked.

"You think you can carry Gill's weight?"

"What?" Gill asked.

"I think so."

"Okay, then. Gill, climb down over Alfonzo and see if you can reach the floor."

"Are you nuts?" Gill cried. "That'll never work!"

"It *will* work," Matt assured him. "I saw someone do it once on a TV show. Just climb down as far as you can and see if you can see more of the room. If you can, maybe you can make it to the floor."

"This is crazy!" Gill protested.

"Would you rather go back up?" Lamar asked him.

"What's my third choice?"

"Look," Matt said, "consider this great practice for doing stunts when you become famous."

After a pause, Gill said, "Okay."

Matt could hear Gill crawling down the ladder, through the shaft. He heard him step on Alfonzo's hand, then his shoulder and down his body. "I hope your pants are on tight!" he said at one point.

A few moments later, Gill reported, "Hey! It worked! I can see something! There are some small lights down here!"

"Can you turn one on?" Matt asked.

"They're already on—they're like . . . computer lights. Like the little green light that comes on when you turn on your computer."

Alfonzo grunted. "Gill! You're getting heavy!"

"I think . . . I can almost . . . AUGH!!"

CRASH!

After a pause, Alfonzo said, "Whoops."

"Gill, you all right?" Lamar asked.

"Yes!" Gill shouted back. "But I think I might be unconscious again!"

"Gill! What does it look like down there?" Matt asked.

"It's a . . . room."

A room? Matt wondered. *Maybe an old administrative office for the mining company?*

FLASH!

At once, the boys were blinded as the shaft filled with a bright light that pierced their eyes.

"AAAAAUUUGHHHH!!!" they all shouted.

"I found the light switch," Gill announced.

When his eyes adjusted, Matt nodded down to Lamar. His friend crawled down, over Alfonzo, and jumped into the room below. Matt was next, and then Alfonzo dropped, too, his friends catching him.

"Good teamwork," he complimented Matt as they put him down. Alfonzo massaged his hands as the four boys stood in the room in wide-eyed wonder.

The floor was as hard as granite, but white and smooth like the tile in their school lunchroom. The walls and ceiling were white, too, with tiny holes

everywhere—like termites had had a heyday . . .
except they were perfectly spaced and perfectly round.
The room was square and large, about the size of the
two-car garage at Matt's house . . . maybe larger.

The room contained several long, brushed steel
tables—just like those in shop class. They had
rounded edges and legs, but no drawers. Sitting on
the surfaces were computer innards—motherboards,
memory modules, and hard drives—all disassembled
and lying around haphazardly. Some were under mag-
nifying glasses; others were sitting on microscope
plates. Still others were stacked in junk boxes, ready
to go out with the garbage. Other electronic parts
were sitting on the tables, too—resistors, capacitors,
and metal films—stuff Matt vaguely remembered
studying in science class. At the back of the tables
were a variety of electronic devices Matt had only
seen in techie movies and boring educational films.
It was the kind of stuff that measured wavelengths
and voltage, displaying the results on little screens.

There were only two chairs in the room. One was
at one of the tables. The other chair was at a desk, also
made of metal. It had no file drawers or cubbyholes,
just four legs and a short surface. A four-drawer, metal
filing cabinet jetted out from the wall beside the desk.
Matt immediately noticed the putty-colored computer
keyboard, trackball, and large computer monitor on

top of the desk. The monitor was the thin kind that could just as easily hang on a wall. The cord from the monitor draped down the back of the desk and attached to a tiny computer tower at the side, with nothing but a CD-ROM drive and a power button. The keyboard and trackball appeared to be wireless. A printer sat beside the computer tower, a stack of printed pages sitting in its tray. Matt noted, as Gill had earlier, that the power lights to the computer and monitor were on, though the computer screen appeared blank.

Finally, above the desk, a simple bulletin board was attached to the wall. Several newspaper clippings were tacked on the bulletin board, along with a plain analog clock ... ticking loudly. *Tick ... tick ... tick ...*

"What is this place?" Lamar asked.

"Looks like some kind of secret bunker or something," Matt guessed.

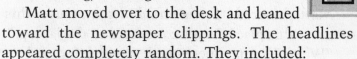

Matt moved over to the desk and leaned toward the newspaper clippings. The headlines appeared completely random. They included:

Train derails in South Bend
Senator Noggin announces early retirement
Promised vaccine passes early testing
Earthquake delays Silicon Valley research

And one more that made Matt's stomach turn:

Enisburg Security Bank robbery foiled

The only common thread was that each story contained adjectives circled in bright red marker. "Amazing" ... "unexpected" ... "miraculous" ... "surprising" ... "fate" ... "startling" ... the list went on. A large, yellow Post-It note caught Matt's attention. It contained four black, block letters:

CIVD

Beside the "D," written in the same red marker, were the letters:

eceit

"C-I-V-Deceit," Matt read, squinting. It made about as much sense as the email that ... "Hey, guys, what was that email address that was listed as connected to the Wordtronix website?"

Lamar had it. "civd@wordtronix.com."

Matt shivered. "I was afraid of that. Guys, this room ... this place ... it's connected to the laptop."

"What?" Lamar questioned, stepping forward.

 "Check it out." Matt pointed to the bulletin board. "It can't be a coincidence. The house, this bunker, C-I-V-D. Somehow it's all connected."

Lamar, Gill, and Alfonzo gathered around Matt and read the cryptic Post-It note.

"What's it mean?" Gill asked.

"I have no idea." Matt looked at the ticking clock. "But I'm sure it'll be revealed in time."

"Well, you wanted some clues," Lamar pointed out. "It looks like you've found some."

Gill reached down and picked up one of the print-outs in the printer tray. As he stood, he bumped the table and the trackball shook. The computer screen flickered as the computer woke up. The screen stayed black, but a dialogue box popped up. It said:

```
Enter password:
```

"What's the password?" Alfonzo asked.

Matt looked at his friends and then typed in:

```
WORDTRONIX
```

The box changed to:

```
Invalid password.

Enter password:
```

"I don't know," Matt said. He looked at the printout— a sheet filled from top to bottom with mathematical formulas. Matt thought it looked like algebra or calculus or physics or something, but he wasn't sure since he hadn't yet studied any of those subjects.

Gill put it back. "This is creepy," he said softly.

"Check *this* out." Lamar knelt at the rear of the computer tower. "Look how this thing is connected to the wall."

Matt looked. A couple of cords extended from the back of the CPU to outlets on the wall.

"This connected to some kind of network?" Matt asked.

Lamar shrugged. "Maybe. It's just . . . I saw a cord like this somewhere. You know what I think? I think it's connected to the Internet."

"Everyone's connected to the Internet," Gill said.

"No," Lamar corrected. "I mean, I think it's a server. So you can access it from anywhere."

"So we might be able to access this computer from my house?" Matt asked.

"Maybe. But we'd have to know the address . . . and, of course, the password."

Matt rubbed his temples. "Well, let's put those items on our 'to do' list." Out of curiosity, he pressed the open button on the CD-ROM drive. It slid open quickly and a glistening CD shined from its tray. Matt pulled it out and looked at it.

"Oh man!" Gill cried.

At once, everyone stood straight up.

"What?" Matt asked.

"There's no way out of here!"

The boys looked around. Gill was right. Oddly enough, there was no door in the room.

"We can go back up the hole," Matt said. "Just like last time. Teamwork."

"Patience," Alfonzo soothed. "There *has* to be another way in here."

The QoolQuad searched the room, but came up empty-handed . . . until Gill tried to open one of the drawers of the tall filing cabinet. Instead of opening, the entire cabinet moved smoothly, sliding aside and revealing a thin passageway.

"Open sesame," Gill whispered. "Who's first?"

The four boys looked at each other. Matt volunteered.

Cautiously, Matt led the troops into the passageway. The deeper into it they walked, the more the passage twisted and the darker it became until they couldn't see where they were going any longer. Matt groped for quite a distance, until they reached the end. From above, a glimmer of light shone down.

> **The deeper into it they walked, the more the passage twisted and the darker it became.**

"Here's a ladder!" Matt announced. He climbed it to the top—about 20 feet—when he hit another grate with a latch. He popped it open and pushed it up. Light flooded in. Matt climbed higher until his head was above the surface. Suddenly, his eyes grew wide and his mouth went dry.

In front of his face was a set of logs. He knew exactly where he was.

In the fireplace.

He was in the fake fireplace of the cabin at RR1, Box 87. No wonder the fireplace didn't have a chimney. It was really a secret passageway.

Matt climbed out and slowly entered the living room. He reached down and helped Lamar, Gill, and Alfonzo out of the passage. As each one entered, they gasped as the puzzle pieces started to fit into place.

They'd found the cabin.

They'd found its true purpose: to hide a secret bunker.

They'd found that the secret bunker was somehow connected to Matt's laptop . . . but that's where the evidence became muddied. Suddenly, Matt found he had more questions than answers.

"Now we're going to jail. My career is over," Gill said flatly. "We're breaking and entering."

"We didn't mean to," Matt assured Gill.

"That doesn't matter," Gill protested. "I've seen Judge Judy. We're toast."

Matt looked at the fireplace mantel and spied the small clock he had seen earlier through the window. It was nothing spectacular. Just a small, square, white clock. But it wasn't working. It had stopped at 11:59:59. One second before midnight.

Across the room was another clock—exactly the same—on a table. It was also stopped a second before midnight. Then Matt noticed another one . . . and another one . . . each on a different wall of the room.

Alfonzo unlocked the dead bolt on the front door. He reached for the doorknob, but Matt grabbed his hand and stopped him cold.

"Wait!" he said, hushed. "Wires." Above the door, four wires spread around the room. Each one led to one of the clocks.

"That an alarm system?" Alfonzo asked.

"I don't think so," Matt said. "But I don't feel good about this. Someone didn't want visitors."

Suddenly, his friend's faces turned ashen-white.

A shadow played across the room, coming from the grimy window by the front door.

Matt's knees began to shake.

A large figure stood outside the door.

The boys stepped back.

They were about to meet the hunter.

Slowly the doorknob twisted.

9

Snap! Crackle! Pop!

The doorknob turned, and Matt felt like he was in slow motion, moving farther back into the house. Should he run to the door and throw the dead bolt? No, no time. He quickly reached into his backpack and pulled out his laptop. He pressed the power button.

BAM! At once, the door flew open like it was made from cardboard. Matt, Lamar, Gill, and Alfonzo looked at the perpetrator. They gasped. The man was *huge.* Anger contorted his face. He was filthy and ugly just like—

"Hulk?!?" Lamar shouted.

Yes, Hulk Hooligan ... after 48 hours without a decent shower.

"What are you doing here?!" Gill shouted at Hulk.

"You guys are in *huge* trouble," Hulk announced.

Snap! The bursting of the door snapped something into motion. Like the lighting of a fuse, the four wires connected to the door ignited. A spark crawled along the wires, dividing into each of the four paths.

Alfonzo tapped Matt on the shoulder. "Um . . . what happens when the sparks hit the clocks?"

"Let's not stick around to find out." Matt threw his laptop, still powering up, back into his backpack. Grabbing Alfonzo and Lamar by the jacket sleeves, he ran toward the door. Gill was right on their tail. Hulk jumped aside and the four boys shot through like bullets out of a gun. They jumped down the porch steps and ran up the hill toward the cave. At the top, they flew over and hit the ground. Then they peeked over the top.

"Hulk!" Matt shouted. The big lug was just standing in the cabin's doorway. "What's he doing?!"

"Hulk!" Lamar shouted, jumping up.

Matt grabbed his arm. "You'll never make it in time."

Gill shook his head. "Timing is everything. You can make it, Lamar."

Matt yanked his laptop out of his backpack. "This is going to take teamwork."

Lamar nodded and took off over the cliff's edge, running to the cabin. Matt's laptop was fully booted now, and he launched the word processor.

Matt watched Lamar jump up the steps and grab Hulk's arm, yelling at him.

Inside the cabin, the wires had surely crackled down and were only inches from the clocks. He typed:

```
Hulk gets off the porch.
```

Matt hit the clock key and the laptop went to work. At the cabin entrance, Lamar pulled, and Hulk stepped forward two paces. He was off the porch and onto the steps.

And there, he stopped.

Matt imagined the wires fizzling behind each clock. He shook his head. He knew he was being too general. His plot needed substance, exact direction, a clear goal. He had to speed the plot up. With seconds to spare, Matt hit the enter key twice and, with flying fingers, he typed:

```
Hulk knew what he wanted. More than
anything else, he wanted freedom. Freedom
from danger. Freedom from stupidity.
```

Matt looked at the cabin. Lamar was still pulling Hulk's arm. Matt smirked and typed:

```
He wanted freedom from Lamar, who jumped on
Hulk's back as if he were the Lone Ranger.
```

Matt hit the clock key. The on-screen cursor changed to a clock, swiftly ticking forward, and then back. Suddenly, Lamar jumped on Hulk's back. Hulk yelled something, Lamar yelled something back, and then Hulk took off down the steps. As the piggyback duo broke into a sprint, Matt knew the clocks around the living room had ticked to midnight ... for suddenly ...

Ka-BOOOOOOOOOMMMM!!!!! Through the open front door, Matt saw fingers of fire shoot out from the four walls of the cabin, straight to the center of the living room. The streams collided like brittle magnets. Then, at once, the house imploded on all four sides, collapsing as if it was created to fold away. Hulk galloped up the hill at top speed, with Lamar on his back. As they began to feel the heat of the explosion, Hulk dove over the cliff. Lamar leaped off his back and crashed into Gill and Alfonzo. Matt slammed his laptop shut and rolled aside.

Smash! The roof crumbled into the cabin, flattening the entire structure. Mounds of white dust poured from the attic, putting out the fire in seconds.

Mash! Behind them, as if somehow connected to the cabin implosion, the entrance to the old cave collapsed into itself, sealing off its treasure inside.

The QoolQuad sat up and looked at each other with question marks on their faces. Obviously, Sam hadn't wanted anyone inside—the reason he set the cabin to implode if anyone entered, hiding the evidence. Matt and his friends had just been fortunate enough to find a rear entrance. But now it was gone . . . forever. Both the front and rear entrances were nothing now but huge mounds of dirt and charred wood. The boys had found more clues than they had ever imagined . . . but now they were all gone. Once again, they were empty-handed.

Then Matt felt a sharp pain in his side. He reached into his jacket pocket and pulled out the object hitting his gut—the CD from the computer in the secret bunker. In all the excitement, he had shoved it in his pocket. The sun winked at him as he turned the CD around in his hand. He smiled. So he had ended up with a clue after all.

"Way to blow up the house," Gill said to Hulk.

"I didn't blow up the house!" Hulk protested. "I just opened the door!"

"Then do me a favor," Gill pleaded. "Don't *ever* open the door to my house."

Matt shoved the CD back into his jacket pocket. "Hey, Hulk," he said, nudging the big guy. "We won't tell anyone if you don't."

Hulk nodded. Then he turned to Lamar. "Man . . . ya . . . ya saved my life." He grabbed Lamar's shoulders and squeezed them tight. "I owe ya big-time!!"

"Oh . . . no . . . you don't . . . really."

"Yeah, I do! I'll figure out some way to repay ya!"

"Oh, please don't."

"Man, how long have you been following us?" Alfonzo asked Hulk.

"Everyone at camp's been looking for ya since yesterday afternoon," Hulk said. "Ya guys are in *such* big trouble."

Matt could just imagine the explosion when they returned to camp. Compared to *that*, this cabin was *nothing*.

"It's not our fault," Matt defended. "We got caught in the current and crashed our canoes."

"I know. We found 'em. Den we all split up." Then, "Ya know I got a dousand splinters tearin' apart dat cave down dere lookin' for ya."

"That was *you?*" Alfonzo asked. "Do you know how bad you scared us? We thought the Lone Ranger was hunting us!"

Hulk guffawed. "Ya guys were stupid."

"Maybe," Matt admitted. "But why did you write 'Wordtronix' everywhere? That spooked us out."

Hulk's face twisted. "I wrote *what?*"

"Wordtronix," Matt repeated.

"I dunno what yer talkin' 'bout, Calhan."

Suddenly, Matt spied Hulk's shoes. Not cowboy boots—tennis shoes. Matt looked at Lamar. Lamar looked at Gill. Gill looked at Alfonzo. Alfonzo looked at Matt. Matt gulped.

"I think we'd better get back to camp," Matt said, returning his laptop to his backpack, "And *fast*. Last one there is a rotten egg roll."

> The handsome knight in dented armor closed his visor. He stared through the holes at the champion, raring to joust against him. He had to win . . . for if he didn't, fair Penelope would be shark bait.

"This is really good, Matt!" Mr. Calahan congratulated his son. He scrolled down the page in the laptop, which was sitting on Matt's lap, to read more.

Matt, Lamar, Gill, Alfonzo, their dads, and Pastor Ruhlen all sat in the back of the bus, riding back to Enisburg, California. Home sweet home. Matt could hardly wait. They all sat in the back, not only because they were so glad to see each other after their adventure, but also because they were quarantined from the rest of the bus.

All four boys and their fathers were covered head-to-toe in white anti-itching lotion. Matt could hardly believe it, but it turned out that somewhere along the way, they'd gotten into some poison oak. Gill wasn't imagining things after all.

Due to the outbreak, camp had ended early.

Now, here they all were, shaking like cans of soda, ready to explode—but not with anger or resentment . . . only thankfulness that they were safely together again. Matt had not written a plot about improving his relationship with his father on this trip . . . but somehow the details took care of themselves.

When the boys had finally made it back to the campsite, Matt had run to his dad, who gave him a huge hug in front of the guys. Matt really hadn't minded that much. He had just been thrilled his dad wasn't mad.

"I'm so glad you're safe," his dad had said. He told Matt he had been worried, and that the entire camp had been up all night searching for the boys. Still, he admitted, somehow he had known Matt and his friends would be all right—he had known they'd use their heads.

"We used teamwork," Matt admitted.

His dad had smiled and ruffed up Matt's hair.

Oddly enough, the trip back upstream to Pete the Pirate hadn't nearly been as tough as Matt had anticipated. He decided to leave the steering to his dad, and he found it much easier to paddle than before. Each stroke had been less of a chore.

As the boys and their fathers laughed in the back of the bus, Matt watched his dad as he read Matt's most recent story on his laptop. He really seemed to be enjoying it. Matt almost hadn't offered to let him read it; he didn't think his dad would be interested. But he took a chance—and his dad seemed delighted. He even laughed a couple times.

And then his cell phone rang. Matt looked at the small device and couldn't believe it. It had been drowned and pitched into the mud, but it still rang. It was the cell phone that would not die. Mr. Calahan pulled it off his belt and looked at the display.

"You have to get that, don't you?" Matt asked, the moment spoiled.

Mr. Calahan stared at the phone. It rang again.

Lamar was right. Matt knew he had to say *something*. It wasn't right to just stay quiet when it bothered him so much. Finally, on the third ring, "Dad, do you ever feel like *not* answering? Like maybe it would be better to throw that thing out the window?"

Mr. Calahan looked at his son for a long moment, then, "You know, I do."

With that, he leaned over, yanked down the closest window and chucked his phone out.

Matt's mouth dropped.

Lamar's mouth dropped.

Gill's mouth dropped.

Alfonzo's mouth dropped.

The phone, traveling at sixty miles per hour, crashed onto the highway, exploding into a few pieces before it was crushed and splattered—without mercy—into a zillion bits, by a sixteen-wheeler.

"WHOA!" everyone shouted, including the dads.

Mr. Calahan calmly closed the window, picked up Matt's laptop, and continued reading.

Matt tapped on his dad's shoulder. "Dad, I think your cell phone is really dead this time."

"Ya think?" Alfonzo asked.

Matt swallowed hard. "Dad, I wasn't serious."

"I was. Seriously awesome."

Matt smiled wide. "Yeah ... "

Lamar nodded to Matt, who nodded back. He had said something to his dad and it had actually worked. Somehow, this weekend, his dad had changed. Maybe he realized his business wasn't as urgent as he once thought. Maybe he realized his family came first.

"But what are you going to do when we get home? You need a phone for work."

Mr. Calahan shrugged. "Matt, this weekend is about *us*. Not our technology. I can always get another phone. But I've only got one son."

"Maybe you could get one with a vibrate feature so it isn't so loud. Oh, and games. Gill's dad has one with games."

Matt's dad laughed. "Yeah, that's not a bad idea. So how about your laptop, Ace?"

Matt looked at his laptop and felt his stomach tighten. Lamar cut him a glance. "You want me to toss my laptop out the window?"

"Yes."

Matt's eyes grew wide as he gulped.

Mr. Calahan laughed again. "*No*, I don't want you to toss it out the window. But how 'bout you let up on it a bit? Not your writing. But next time you go canoeing, how 'bout leaving it onshore?"

Matt nodded, running his hand along the side of the laptop. "I guess I have been a little ... preoccupied with it."

Mr. Calahan roughed up Matt's hair. "Happens to the best of us." Then, without another word, he leaned in and read the rest of the story.

"So what happens next?" Mr. Calahan asked when he reached the end.

Matt shrugged. "Well, I'm not sure. I haven't developed the plot that far."

"The plot, huh? You really have the talent for this stuff. It doesn't make a lick of sense to me."

"Well, the plot is like the substance of the story," Matt explained. "It's an exact direction. A clear goal. Without a good plot, a story just falls flat."

Mr. Calahan nodded. "So the plot's like the foundation and then you have to build the story structure upon it, huh?"

Matt smiled. Leave it to his dad to bring it down to construction terms. Maybe they had more in common than he thought. "Exactly."

"So after you have the plot, what do you do?"

"Well, I try to create good characters—support beams—to make the story stand on its own."

Mr. Calahan nodded. "So what about this story? What happens next?" he asked again.

"I'll leave that to the characters. That way, there could be a surprise right around the corner."

"True," his dad said. "Then again, sometimes it's better not to have surprises when you're building. Have you thought about putting together a blueprint?"

"You mean an outline?"

"Yeah, an outline. It's like this . . . "

And for the rest of the trip, Matt and his dad talked about writing and construction. A week ago, Matt would have never imagined it. But that's what Matt loved about being a writer. Whenever life threw him a "What-if?" scenario, he was ready for it. *What if Dad and I actually have something in common?* he wondered. Only time would tell.

Until then, the laptop was still the QoolQuad's secret. But Matt imagined that if his dad *did* discover his secret one day, it wouldn't be such a bad scenario. For he'd heard that between a young man and his mentor the secrets of life are always revealed in time. Matt could hardly wait.

Epilogue

"Matt!" Gill shouted, bursting into Matt's room.

Matt put up his hand, signaling Gill to be quiet for a moment. He was staring closely at his laptop.

"What's that?" Gill asked, looking at the screen. It was filled with a muddied picture composed of gray and black boxes.

"I think," Matt answered, "that it's a satellite photo. Of what, I don't know. This is what was on the CD."

"That's it?" Gill asked.

"That's it. One picture file. I don't even know if it's important." Matt pointed to one corner. "I think this is a sign on a building—a logo of some kind. Have you ever seen it anywhere?"

Gill squinted, but couldn't make it out. "You mean that little blur on the big blur?"

Matt shook his hands in the air. "This is so frustrating! We nearly drowned, we got lost, we got chased, we blew up a house, and what do we have to show for it?"

Gill shrugged and scratched his arm. "We got a day off school. The whole trip was worth it for the poison oak."

"Gill!"

"Hey, do I need to remind you that I didn't want to be Super Stunt Adventure Guy in the first place? I don't like being chased."

"You know, I've been thinking about that," Matt said. "Someone out there was following us for two days straight. They chased us and scared us, but they never really did anything to us."

"What are you saying?"

Matt shrugged. "I don't know. It's like . . . someone was just testing us or something. Trying to see how we'd react."

Gill chewed on the idea for a moment and nodded thoughtfully. "Well, it wasn't a complete waste. You got a satellite photo of a small blur on a big blur. I'm sure now that you have *that*, everything will start to fall into place."

"Are you being sarcastic?"

"*Me?*"

"You can go home now."

Then Gill sniffed the air. He grimaced and asked, "What's that smell?"

"I didn't do it," Matt quickly retorted.

"No," Gill clarified. "It smells like . . . *perfume*."

The corner of Matt's mouth upturned, but he quickly wiped it away. "Mom says Isabel stayed in my room while she was here. Everything smells like that." Matt closed his eyes and took a deep breath. "My bathroom, my pillow, my beanbag . . ."

Gill unlatched the window above Matt's desk. "Well, let's air this place out, man!"

Matt caught Gill's hand. "No, um . . . the wind might make it . . . stronger. Wouldn't want that."

 Gill's right eyebrow jumped up. He wasn't buying it.

"So," Matt said, changing the subject. "What's up?"

Gill suddenly jumped. "Oh! Matt, you've *got* to help!" Matt rolled his eyes and turned around in his desk chair. His red-haired friend had concern written all over his face.

"What do you need help with? Nothing with your dad again, I hope."

"Look, I just found out about the commercial part I got—it's for advertising a snack!"

"Great! So you won't even have to act. Who doesn't like snacks?"

"Guess *which* snack?"

Matt shrugged.

"It's for Pooka Dookas! *Pooka Dookas make-a you puke-a!*" he emphasized. Then, "Matt . . . stop laughing."

Matt couldn't help himself. "You're kidding, right? I mean, how could it be any worse?"

"Matt, I don't think I can do it. I need your laptop's help."

"I don't know, Gill . . . "

"It's to make my dreams come true."

"Pooka Dookas?"

"YES! Ugh!"

Matt nodded. "OK, I'll help a little bit—if needed."

"Thank you!" Gill exclaimed. "I promise: You won't regret it."

Matt took a deep breath. "Now why does that make me nervous?"

To be continued . . .

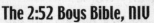

The 2:52 Boys Bible, NIV

General Editor, Rick Osborne

Helping boys ages 8 to 12 become more like Jesus mentally, physically, spiritually, and socially – Smarter, Stronger, Deeper, and Cooler!

Hardcover 0-310-70320-4
Softcover 0-310-70552-5

Laptop 4: Power Play

Written by Christopher P. N. Maselli

Softcover 0-310-70341-7

Techno thrillers that will keep you on the edge of your seat – 2:52 Soul Gear™ Laptop fiction books!

Bible Heroes & Bad Guys

Written by Rick Osborne

Softcover 0-310-70322-0

Comic book action straight from the pages of the Bible – 2:52 Soul Gear™ non-fiction books!

Zonder**kidz**®